PLANET
POLYGAMOUS

PLANET POLYGAMOUS

SHINIE ANTONY

INDIALOG PUBLICATIONS PVT. LTD.

Published in August 2005

Indialog Publications Pvt. Ltd.
O - 22, Lajpat Nagar II
New Delhi - 110024
Ph.: 91-11-29830504
Fax: 91-11-29835221
www.indialog.co.in

10 9 8 7 6 5 4 3 2 1

Printed at Print Tech, New Delhi.

ISBN 81-87981-92-X

For Stella, the most edible aunt in the world

Contents

ACKNOWLEDGEMENTS

Rupali Thapar
Vandana Pulapaka
Rama Varma
Sangeeta Singh
Humra Quraishi
Vandana Chatterjee
G. Sampath
Debasmita Majumdar
Suvadip Sinha
Mita Ghose
Shruti Susan Rajan
Debashish Mukerji

How I missed her, how I missed her,
How I missed my Clementine...
So I kissed her little sister
And forgot my Clementine

SITTING DUCKS

Photographs lie. Look at this one; the girl is turned bashfully toward the camera, a twinkle poised between eye and lip so that you begin to smile in return, and that lacy petticoat hem ready to swish at the slightest breeze. There's a kitten, too, whose mewling breath you almost hear whoosh into her ankles. And the table she leans against, an inanimate limb of timber she grips for support, only reinforces her predisposition for motion, to sway, to be distracted by a cycle-bell, milk boiling over, a noise in the lane behind; it binds her there momentarily to blindly blink at the flash-bulb, the light bleaching her for just that instant, shackling her in its solemn sepia archives as this young girl, at this bright moment, here and now, *alive*.

In reality Geetanjali has been dead a good fifty years. The memory of her touch lingered lighter and lighter until one day it had vanished altogether, the annals of her short, short life not hovering in the air even on the annual occasions of birth or death anniversaries. The picture hung on a rusted nail out on the wall that could be spied through the grill by outsiders, pesky beggars or neighbourhood children playing hide and seek, almost a part of the wall it dangled on, the wall and the frame both beige with age, on a house once named after her....

A granddaughter of the current owner of the house was brought retching and vomiting from school. Medicines, alternative and allopathic, failed to stem nausea and the little girl of eight turned all skin and raggedy bones before their eyes.

"She is the baby of the house, the burning lamp," announced her incoherent mother, "Do something before ... before...."

Everyone knew how the sentence would end; before Meetu lived on in photographs on walls. A new option was tentatively suggested.

"It can't harm," they whispered. "Doctors say it is genetic and have washed their hands off. Let's ask Lalaji."

Lalaji's subsequent nod summoned a tantrik with long jet-black locks teasing the back of his neck, but with clothes ordinary enough to warrant sighs of relief.

He walked around Meetu's bed three times holding

a candle. When the flickering flame went out and the naked wick sizzled, he told them, "See."

They nodded mutely though privately they blamed the breeze, the fan's disobedient blades and each other's breath for the flame's exit.

"Is there any penance to be done in this house?"

"Yes," screamed Meetu's mother. "They don't talk about it, but a girl in this family was sacrificed long ago."

"The woman is beside herself with sorrow," her father-in-law apologized. "There were no killings here, only the natural demise of my little sister."

The tantrik bade that women leave the room, all except Meetu, who by virtue of her unconsciousness was allowed to stay put. "A virgin, right, before puberty?"

"Er, yes," Lalaji said, not having thought of his sister for a long time, let alone in menstrual terms.

"How old was she exactly?"

The brother did a hasty calculation, muttering, "The year of flood, the month of Durga…" etc. And then, "Nine years and three months."

"That was no accident," pronounced the tantrik sternly, ten presumably the cut-off age for human sacrifices.

He was fed, watered, paid and dismissed in the same lacklustre way as the city doctors but the head of the house now slept less. When the jasmine creepers let loose their clichéd fragrance or the moon routinely peek-a-booed among clouds, Lalaji tossed on his mat, the starch in his pillowcase somehow reminiscent of the sea. He couldn't sleep, that was the truth, not when dreams made such a din!

And in the quiet he could hear too the dwindling of his granddaughter, the ebbing of her life despite an eye-watering *havan* where prayers were offered and holy red threads tied around wrists, and as surely as he had prospered and multiplied in the carbolic soap business, he knew they were going to lose her. It was in the blood, this conclusion, flowing from womb to womb till it had come to her and stood still.

In that peculiar dusk to dawn corridor, the house around him grew young and he was transported to his own life a long time ago, before his wife who had died of a heart attack six years ago came into his life, even before adolescence really, when all he cared for were good hiding places for the stolen sweetmeats he had smuggled into his room as his mother groaned in the basement, permanently being delivered of babies.

Prayers were routinely offered to the reigning deities since Lalaji had no female sibling and his parents were rabid for a daughter. A sea of boys till the eye could see and the eye ached to spy some feminine razzmatazz for a change. Roughly two years into his teenage and an in-house stay by Babaji, a patchy-skinned saffron-clad sanyasi, they were finally blessed with a baby girl and his mother could heave a sigh of relief and retire from the business of childbirth via the time-tested method of celibacy.

The baby was bathed in milk and rosewater, powdered with ivory dust and fussed over endlessly. Lalaji never forgot his first glimpse of her in the ornate crib; a scrawny scrap of pure ape, he had thought.

As she grew it was obvious she resembled no one in the immediate family and her fair skin, a continuing delight, raised hyperbole. The sprite graced most laps, paternal, maternal, relatives and guests; no one put her down for long.

Those days, when calling a photographer was high expense and synonymous with celebrations, she was a perennial model of parental pride and extravagance. The boys were photographed upon their graduation and weddings (though Lalaji hated the exclusive footage of him in his Convent choir with mouth miming an improbable soprano in the back row), but she was there in many a solo frame, in myriad contrived moods. What Lalaji particularly and rancorously remembered was the gaiety that followed the reception of the photographs, the high-strung hum of praise, the happy arguing over framing, hanging, etc, which transcended mere adulation. It was like they wanted her to stay small and lisping forever, be their immortal infant as they aged and withered worshipfully around her.

The adoration, which irritated the boys not a little, when it ended, ended so abruptly that it failed to

convey the joy they had anticipated. Lalaji remembered
creeping into the house in the hours of early dawn,
having spent the night with his friends smoking and
coughing, and though all was silent and hushed, he
still felt a chill like a scythe split his spine in two.
What alerted him to the absence of the all-pervading
sense of affection that always hung in the air ever since
the last child was born he couldn't say, but it was there,
the sudden severance.

A trusted servant whispered to him, "See those
white patches," and he saw them.

Both parents with alarming rapidity withdrew from
family life and by the time Lalaji returned from his
first foreign sojourn to Ceylon, Geetanjali was often
found roaming in solitary splendor, unwashed and
unlettered, hobnobbing with servants and mangy
felines. All photographs duly vacated the walls, except
that one in the front, owing to oversight or sheer
apathy.

Before Lalaji left for Burma on a dank night to
secure a retail tie-up, he heard his father stumble
drunkenly up the stairs, his murmurs loud and clear
in the still night air. "Some stranger's seed passed off
as mine. Can't tolerate…." Followed by a hissing "slut"
at his mother's door before the faltering footsteps
reached their own room.

"Son," his father addressed him when Lalaji had
ambled in with studied casualness to help. "You know
the property papers … get them for me, and that Vakil

chap. Changes are needed, you understand, don't you? You seem old enough."

Lalaji scrutinized the dispossessed, disinherited girl, an interloper after whom this whole house had been renamed with such misplaced pomp, this girl scrubbing dirt into a linen-white cheek, scavenging for similarities. The savage patches of paternity had fanned out to neck and shoulders like pinned badges and she cowered instinctively when she saw him.

"What are you doing?" he gentled.

"It is m … milk," she stammered, unused to attention anymore. "Milk has left marks on me like cat's paws."

He knew she had been trying to rub away those telltale spots, to worm her way back into the family. But his kindness, the sort one felt for an outsider, obliterated before it could form depth or degrees, and he turned away, reminding himself to call the lawyer and turn heritage to his own advantage.

She must have thrown up, must have boiled over with fever too before she succumbed, who knew, Lalaji thought now lying on his mat. He couldn't remember the details with any clarity.

Moonbeams pressed against his eyelids like hot rods, reminding him of the night he carried her limp body past the iron gates – the same gates that she used to swing on in happier times, her childish chuckle trailing majestically after her – and bade the pyre shut midway since there was no use wasting the fine sandalwood that family honour had necessitated, consigning the half-burnt body to backwater foam.

Lalaji uncorked a futile antibiotic tube. Absently, he rubbed the ripples of paleness on his arms while the odour of seaweed grew stronger.

DAYDREAM AT 3.30 A.M.

I am not the arty type, but all the same I walked into that art gallery.

Having reached half an hour early for a lunch date with a former colleague, I had targeted the fancy bathroom for time-pass but a shot-in-the-heart sanitary napkin lay bleeding in the bin, hurrying me out of there and into the hotel's basement to look at overpriced wares.

And then I saw the gallery and walked in without a conscious thought except a fervent hope that the clock would hurry. I was to meet this real blabbermouth and I was dying to know how the office had moved on, or rather not moved on, after I quit for a better position last month. Not that the intrinsic nature of my job had changed at all. I still hung around the boss's desk, peering into his PC with the most humble expression in the world.

A small dais in a corner said "Photos" and since I am a short person and by habit attracted to higher platforms, I climbed to take a look. As usual, they were black and white portraits of disasters and tragedies. Emaciated women and children stared back at me with large accusing eyes, imbuing my casualness almost with arrogance. It was only the picture of a half-dead man being buried that caught my complete attention. Skinny, all bones and eyes, he was being pushed into a hole in the ground by what looked like uniformed men. Which country, what year, nothing was included in the caption, which simply said, "Buried Alive."

His eyes were surprisingly open and fixed on me like I was the death that came at him untold, uninvited, slow inch by slow inch. I wondered idly if this picture wasn't somebody's nightmare. For say, someone who loved him and whom he loved in return, someone whose heart and dreams were broken by his death. I shivered at a nip in the air and looked round questioningly if someone had tampered with the AC.

A little barefoot girl sold balloons next. I had to smile as her balloons were just swept away by the wind. The camera had caught her before despair, with a rounded "o" of surprise on her face. I smiled but remembering the last picture I felt guilty enough to wipe it off immediately. Soon it was time to meet my friend. When I reached the far end of the gallery I felt a pull. It was that man. From that far I could barely make out any details except those extraordinary eyes.

I live alone. I had got the place cheap since it was an illegal construction on the terrace and had only one room to speak of really. A tiny kitchenette and a tinier bathroom completed the ensemble. Despite the smallness of space, I was vain about it belonging completely to me. It was mine. Others in the building were a faceless blur to me. Some watched me with suspicion, especially Mrs Sharma whose husband beat her almost every night if the *press-walee* was to be believed. A young unmarried woman like me, they were sure, was a whore. If one man did not keep me, then I must be giving myself to all men is the logic tightening their lips as they pass me by on the stairs, exaggeratedly giving me more space than my small form requires.

On Saturday evening I was enjoying my huge terrace, waiting for the stars to come out, thinking of the man I could find irresistible some day. There was someone my Manhattan cousin said might be my type....

But why would I be in a hurry to turn housewife when I was housewife already as sub-editor. The man dragged in the news story; I cleaned it, cooked it and served it but he still got the byline! So I e-mailed an "hmmm" to my cousin. My dream man, the one who'd melt my bones in one orthopaedic swoop, was as far away as the stars that night with Fate yet to google him for me.

It was turning chilly. Autumn had tossed the sidewalks into salad bowls of swirling browns and greens. Sighing, I gathered my teacup and retired inside. Even after closing the door and bolting it, I felt … funny. As if someone was watching me. Watching! That Manhattan guy, may be, I mocked myself. Hey wake up, there's no one waiting for you, Okay? I shook myself. It is all the goose bumps I get living alone.

But everything I did, everywhere I turned, I felt self-conscious. My blood strummed, but who had cried wolf in these veins of mine?

A paper moved, the rustle so deliberate it made me jump. Calm down, I told myself, but I stood still. It was almost like there was someone in the room. Someone who had entered it for the first time and was curious about things in the room. Like he or she was walking around, acquainting self with the room.

Then the telephone rang, startling me. For a moment I was tempted to apologize to my unseen guest, to ignore the ring. Then I laughed at myself and picked up the phone. It was my mother. I lay down on my bed on the floor while talking to her and her mundane homey details soon had a soporific effect on me. Yawning I snuggled into my soft, soft bed, so sleepy I could barely place the receiver back.

I woke up then. Suddenly. *For no reason.* As if someone had woken me up. There was too much light in the room was my first thought. And yes, the curtains were not drawn, causing the moonlight to spill into my room almost like sunshine. Didn't I close the curtains, I asked myself groggily. I never forget to do this usually, do it almost automatically as I have a fear of being watched while sleeping. And for a minute there, just before I came awake so completely, for a minute there I had been transported back to my home in sweet Shillong, when mother used to open the curtains in the morning and I'd groan at the tangy rays. It had been that hiss of curtains sliding across plastic rods as they came apart that woke me I am sure.

Now, now, you'd think I was barmy. I mean who'd come into my room, open my windows, pull back the curtains? No one. Right, so I turned my face into the pillow and slept on.

Only to wake again when all the electric lights in my room came on at once. Stupidly, I stared around at the unbearable brightness stabbing the familiar objects in my room. They all seemed as foreign as a stranger's things at that moment. Must tell the landlord about faulty switches, I thought. Since it was almost morning – the clock said it was after 3 – I unlatched my door and went to the bathroom at the opposite end of the terrace. Before I opened the door, a clanking noise came from inside the bathroom, like the tin bucket in there had been shaken. This gave me quite a fright I can tell you. I ran back into my room and bolted my door quick. Then I stood there breathing hard and feeling very, very foolish. That was when I heard the second set of nostrils. I stopped my own breath to test. Yes, there was something in the room and it was breathing!

"Who is it?" I asked aloud, my voice jerky.

I felt as if something was struggling to articulate.

"If there is someone, give me some indication of your presence," I ordered bravely, despite knowing that any spirit manifestations would cause me to lose all consciousness. But overriding a fear of the unknown was my desperate need to know.

The strange silence continued. I was waiting, but somebody else seemed to be waiting, too.

Well, two can play the game, I thought with abrupt bravado. And with all lights on, I prepared to get back into bed. I had just dozed off again, when I felt a gentle tug at my sheet. That did it. Shrieking, I ran out of my room and leapt down the stairs to stand incoherently at the Sharmas' door. I rang their doorbell in urgent long presses. Mr Sharma opened the door with his customary scowl. And when he saw me, in my oversized T and vertical hair, he almost shut the door. But I threw back his door and rushed into his drawing room.

"There is someone there," I told him between gasps. "Call someone. Get him out. Please."

They have given me this new room. One side is completely glass and I can see the nurses in their white skirts chat with each other or pick up the phone. They tell me this room is very safe and that no one, *no one,* can enter it without them noticing. In the night I switch off my light, but their light is on and it is almost like day out there.

I sleep most of the time since I get very tired. My mother is somewhere nearby. She comes every day with fruits and combs my hair. My cell phone is with her because the first night here, I got a call. I knew who it was. He knew who he was. But he can't talk, you see. For some reason he just won't talk.

But I know he comes, though I don't tell anyone about it anymore. He comes to me here too where they tell me no one can come in without signing the visitor's register. I wake up when the night is bathed in the most beautiful brightness, when the crazy cosmic racism of a light so white dyes the inside of my eye.

And I ache.

Not with painful joints or anything explicable but with a throb in parenthesis, like someone cupped bliss in a palm and was about to blow it at me. I can't explain, except that I am not anxious or scared.

Just aching.

STORY BEST UNTOLD

The rain leapt into her tiny flat with the ferocity of a wedding band. She hated this about Delhi, its moody weather, as if climatic extremities were not irritants enough. Of having to shut windows and blinds in case of dust storms and drizzles, or interiors going too warm or icy cold, of picking one's way amongst the seasonal junk overflowing into the narrow tapered spaces of balcony or corridor, filling up like bowels when one wasn't looking.

Ragini adjusted the plastic awning, sheathing saplings and stunted cacti, watching water lash at other balconies, at clothes topsy-turvying on washing lines, at TV aerials trying to shake loose their concrete roots, goose-pimpled birds huddling under sunshades and what was that – she squinted her eyes against the dim wattage of the sun – a dark shape squatting over the terrace's rim?

The apartment opposite had fifteen floors; a jump would translate into instant death. Ragini hesitated, loath to break the monotony of an artificially whipped up afternoon, a long sedate life up to middle age and menopause untouched by emotional outpourings or human hands. Then before she could think too much and intellectualize first impulses, she picked up an umbrella and made for the door.

It took all of five minutes to make her way to the opposite terrace and she half-hoped he'd have decided by then whether to dip or not to his death and save her from her own nobility. She straggled up a cement culvert to the roof and contemplated tattered kites and other sewage from the sky before visually locating the imbecile who had culled her from her desiccated existence.

"Hey," she shouted but what with the steady downpour it was only when she tapped his crouched shoulder that he noticed her. Then he nodded calmly like he had been expecting her.

"Are you mad?"

"I am only killing myself," he pointed out politely.

"That is a road down below. You could fall on others, taking them with you, or at least crippling them. Plus no one would rent this apartment or buy a flat here and this whole area will swarm with police and press personnel for days and gain a notoriety and low resale value only you can deny."

He blinked. "You don't expect me to care!"

"Do tell," she said conversationally. "Is it lo-ove?"

He snorted. "In a small town everyone gropes everyone, marries everyone, cheats on everyone and in a microcosm, it could appear momentous, but no I wouldn't disintegrate for lo-ove."

"Nothing wrong with that surely?"

He threw her a shrewd glance. "I guess not. Except that...."

"Except what?"

"It is like saying I will not shit again. Love, shit," he shrugged, "The body returns to it again and again."

So much for romance, she thought, consciously keeping her eyes off his bare toes webbed out on the slippery parapet. "If it's neither courage nor cowardice, but the only non-negotiable exit left, you'd better tell me about it."

He considered her impassively. "What good will it do, telling you?"

She settled comfortably against the asphalt, drenched to the bone just as he was, the bedraggled umbrella long ago having turned turtle. "Nothing if goodness is your prime concern. But I do have all the time in the world."

"Your smile ... it lacks dimples."

Then, executing an abrupt turnaround so that his heels hung out in space, he faced her. "You are right. I will tell you so that someone will know, though I don't know you from...."

"Friends call me Rags," she supplied quickly. Rags was what elderly women hung up on their misplaced youth had christened her at her workplace. She flashed her non-dimples. "Just so you know, I have nothing against mortality per se. One does tend to overlook the biodegradable quality of bodies."

He smiled faintly, flexed his Velcroed toes. "Theories make sense only as you mouth them. Stop moving lips and, pffft, they disappear. Listen."

Long hours at office and lack of contemporary cognizance of a woman's mounting weight in the marital scales led him and his wife to predictably part ways. Perhaps there were tears on her side or his, he can't really remember.

There being no formal divorce, the baby she consequently conceived was presumed to be his and he couldn't bring himself to protest against this supposition as long as she didn't dare touch him for support or alimony.

For nineteen years this wife of his was consigned to a murky past, a thimble-full of traumatic memories like everyone else's, a minute detail in his life he had failed to tweak into place, and if he had been informed of her death by post or phone he'd have gone ahead and lived his day no different from other days, glad only of a sense of closure.

However, his bedridden mother-in-law dumped the child a year ago with his own mother, hammering him into a peculiar hell.

"I have a granddaughter and I know now, almost at my deathbed. I am only a mother, why tell me, right?" she screamed hoarsely down the phone.

"Where is my so-called wife?" he asked patiently, overriding the histrionics.

"You don't know? She is abroad. Geneva, isn't it? Some UN project. Anyway, I am glad her other grandmother has generously loaned the child to me."

But, tending to adolescent hulk brought on the grandparental heebie-jeebies and he found himself mouthing an offer of his services. Not that impurity impelled him right from the outset though there was a vague sense of mischief, of belated revenge rife within him. The old rancour he thought dead had merely been hibernating and now was up and about like the devil, brandishing horns and a tail. In his rearranged memories he had become the saint and she the sinner. He would show that woman, he had thought, but that was prioritizing.

The girl was big for her age, addicted to junk food and the TV set. It irked him to return from office and watch her broad shoulders shake with mirth at the animated antics on screen, jaw masticating mechanically. Ire turned to resignation, making the arrangement with its non-specific details somewhat bearable. The haze took a while to clear, a while that the two utilized to the best of their ignorance. Only her precocious pregnancy took him unawares but that decided his vengeance.

He would not take responsibility and his wife would be trapped, having touted this alien obesity as his own seed. Wouldn't be able to wriggle out of *this* baby so easily! He calculated that her return two months hence would coincide with medical refusal to terminate the pregnancy, so far gone would it be.

"You have listening eyes, Rags," he said.

Ragini blinked, shaking off her audience stupor. "I am worried that lightning will finish you off and take all the credit." A pause later she asked, "So did you convince her about the baby?"

Their eyes snarled up then; his maimed by memories, hers suddenly growing spacious. He nodded, banging shut every high-rise window in self-conglomerating angst, for it was he, instead, who had been convinced about a baby long ago.

"I am father to my grandchild," he murmured to himself, spreading hands sideways like wings.

Ragini turned one-eighty degrees in the fraction of a trance, fully focused on securing a wayward umbrella that insisted on darting every which way. And when she reached ground floor and heard the thudding splash, cars screech to a halt and a sudden mob exhale its matted breath, she continued to straighten the black umbrella.

Sometimes, death needs no footnotes. For what of life does one understand at the end except that sooner or later it ... ends.

THE DOLL'S DILEMMA

"Are they twins?" Mala asked. She was like that, easily excited. That, in fact, was the best thing about her. I remember when she first saw me, how her face had glowed.

"Mommy, tell me, no. Are they twins?"

Mala's mother snorted. "I don't know. Just behave yourself. They are, after all, the children of your father's boss."

And off she went to organize the pastries and drinks. She hated it when someone ate at her place and did not ask, "From where did you get *these*? They are heavenly/delicious/the best!"

She wouldn't say anything at the time, just smile slightly. But later she may allow Maya to hug her and not notice how dirty I am.

"Twins! Did you hear that, Dolly?" Mala jabbered to me. There was nothing she did not tell me.

I tried to smile back enthusiastically, but I was thinking how where I was born, there had been hundreds like me, with the same pink frocks and button eyes. We had been hundreds of twins there.

Of course, I was lucky to meet Mala almost immediately.

That evening, the sisters came. They were twins, but sadly for Mala, not identical. Being a well brought up child, though, she dealt bravely with her disappointment.

One of the girls pointed at me, hooting. "You have a doll!"

Mala's mouth wobbled. "No, no," she said. "This is an old one we have kept around just so some baby visitor can play with her."

"Her? You call it a her?"

"See, I have a new computer game," Mala distracted them and I heaved a sigh of relief. I hated to see her put in a spot like that. At nights when she hugged me, she always apologized for such insensitivities on others' part. Even her mother hated to see her dress me up, or sing to me. "Go out and play," she'd yell at Mala.

There was a woman employed just to play with Mala the whole day. Sometimes, when Mala's mother's friends came home, she'd say, "Baby ko leke jao." And we'd all troop out, with me perched on Mala's hip.

Outside, in the parking lot the woman chatted with other maids while Mala chatted with me.

Once, just once, Mala's mother stopped her from taking me along. Mala missed me so much she cried all the time she was out and I missed her, too, especially when immediately after Mala left, Mala's mother burst into tears and told the guest how difficult everything was ever since she had a child. But wait until you hear what happened next. When Mala's mother went in to change, he blew his nose with me. The indignity of it!

Next day, sure enough, Mala's mother yelled again how dirty I was. She is always dunking me in the washing machine. I don't mind the hygiene, but she could wait at least until Mala was in school. She cries each time I go into the machine. She presses her nose against the glass while I go round and round in the soapy water.

These washes keep me clean and I am happy to be clean but they also exhaust me. My hair and clothes get raggedy each time. Not that Mala minds and she is the only one I want to please. But in the last wash my mouth came off. My mouth! It was actually a red thread stitched above my chin in a broad 'U' to make it appear like I am always smiling, which is why I couldn't stop grinning even when that man blew his nose in me.

But whenever Mala came home from school or her parents went out leaving her alone, she'd always look at me and smile. I was always smiling, you see. But with that red thread gone, I looked surly. Or sad.

Mala noticed it straightaway. "Dolly's lost her lips!" she cried. The ayah started to laugh at that. What's so funny, I wondered. Would she laugh if it happened to her? Could she laugh at all without her lips?

Mala's parents had gone for a party. Mala's mother went to and came back from the parties happy. She always mentioned meeting at least three people who did not – would not – just could not – believe she had a child.

It was midnight when Mala's parents finally came home that night. She had waited up for them, just so she could tell them about my lost smile.

"Mama, papa," she called.

When they did not respond, she went to their bedroom, saying, "Let's take Dolly to the hospital."

Mala's father glared at her. "Why aren't you asleep?" Then he glared at his wife. "She doesn't look like me at all. One of these days I'll get the truth out of you, if I have to kill you."

"Go away," Mala's mother told us. She did not look happy.

Ayah has been asked to leave. She was caught stealing, Mala's mother said. But she told the cook and the cook told Mala that Mala's father had hugged ayah, which is why Mala's mother told her to go.

Ayah packed her small bag and was about to leave.

She had reached the door when she noticed me in the foyer. Mala leaves me leaning there on the mantelpiece, so that I am the first one she sees on opening the door when she comes back from school. From here she carries me to the dining room where I watch her eat. Then she puts me in a pram and wheels me about, telling me in detail every single thing she did since she left home. There is even a small cradle, in which Mala rocks me to and fro. She always sings while doing this.

Ayah stood there looking at me for a long while and I wished I could smile goodbye. Then she walked toward me and very deliberately she plucked out my eyes. Yes, my eyes! After that my world went black.

I am one of those dolls without nose or eyebrows to begin with, so lips and eyes were all I had and now they were gone. I sat there blindly waiting for Mala, waiting for light.

Ages later, I heard the door open. It was Mala's mother. She called out to the cook. "Woh gayi?" She meant Ayah. The cook must have nodded as I did not hear her speak.

Then Mala's mother muttered, "This doll, I tell you. What a nuisance. Why can't Mala play with her Barbies for whom I pay a bomb? Why must she drag this ugly thing all over the place, making me a laughing stock?"

"Throw it out before Mala comes," she told the cook. "Tell her the maid stole it."

I am in a plastic bag. Damp tealeaves and rotting coriander stems cling to me everywhere. Then the plastic bag begins to rock to and fro like the cradle Mala sometimes puts me in. Where is the cook taking me, I wondered. And then it struck me.

There have been dark whispers about such places in the toy factory. That this was how we dolls met our end. That we all met in the municipality garbage dump in the end. I did not want to go there. I wanted to meet Mala.

"How baby cried!" I hear the cook say to someone. "But they got her another doll from Singapore. Such blue-blue eyes and golden hair."

My last thought as I sail into the black hole is that Mala would *never* forget meeeeeeeeeeeeee.

SALT AND PEPPER

The old woman let go of her nephew's finger in the park and he shot bang on to the seesaw like an arrow twanged from Eklavyan's own bow, that guy with the disposable thumb.

"Ammooma," he chortled. It was her cue to press down the other end of the seesaw with both her elbows, bringing it down so that his chubby legs dangled in the air.

As her grandson rediscovered old turf, the old woman threw backward glances at the park's gate. At last another old woman appeared there. She was accompanied by two tiny tornadoes who abandoned her almost immediately and clambered on to the carousel with all the solemnity of NASA astronauts being launched into outer space.

"Namaskaram," said one woman to the other and they sank down on the stone bench, hands on knees.

Pleasantries consisted of daughter-in-law updates, one working, one not. The latter consumed most of the discussion owing to the time available to her for perpetuation of domestic warfare. This irked the other mother-in-law somewhat, whose bahu had now taken to cooking entire meals before leaving for office, the witch!

"I saw your daughter-in-law yesterday, reading the newspaper in your balcony, sitting with one leg over the other."

"I told you! Always, one leg over the other like she may lose the battle with her bladder any minute. These non-Brahmins."

The pettiest, the smallest, the tiniest detail was aired, nothing left unsaid or under-spoken for fear of obfuscating the course of insight; this was the salt of their harmony, the common core that pulled them to this park, this empathy, this magnetized bench.

"You know she has cancer."

This brought the winning woman's tongue to a total standstill. Eyes moist, she whispered. "Yes, I know."

They were silent for two whole minutes while the park's acoustics took on a surreal echo; crows cawing contradictorily to bigger crows, the children laughing too loud and swings going berserk on their rusty chains.

"There is no hope, doctors have given up. And her husband doesn't know, poor thing."

The other sighed. "He must have reached Dubai by now."

"They'll ring him up, ask him to return immediately."

"He doesn't know," the murmur was reiterated as they both imagined the soon to be bereaved spouse retracing his steps in the sky, worst suspicions confirmed when he landed.

"He won't be able to take it."

"Oh, he'll take up with that obvious sister of hers. She's always playing pallu politics, demarcating the bosom into %. He'll go squint-eyed just keeping track."

The other woman nodded understandingly, absently twisting the antique watch on her wrist. "The next episode is only an hour away."

BEHOLDER'S EYE

Crank calls and doorbells going at odd hours in the night, these were the price for bargain realty in a lousy locality. Suffice it to say I can prance wet right inside my home if it rains, roof rather in the realm of virtual reality.

"Mom, are you talking to yourself again?" my twelve-year-old daughter asked world-wearily. My divorce has had this effect on most people, convinced them of their superiority over me.

Thank god my ex-husband hadn't wanted this crabby old jalopy; life with its innumerable bum-jobs would've been hell sans mobility. Of course, the car stops without consulting me so that I am constantly apologizing to supercilious men at traffic lights.

"No, I am not colour-blind," I'd mutter, smiling a ditsy, less-literate-than-you smile to mollify them and their feet in the virile act of braking. That was one thing I learnt in my sixteen years of marriage; how to bow and scrape your way out of potential jams before the whole thing blows up in your face. Sometimes, your timing is off and it blows up and your face is right there in the thick of things, of course. Still, you can call it my core competence, this ability to ingratiate my way out.

"Mommeeee," drawled the rapidly growing child next to me, her exaggerated decibels adjusting my sense of proportion and rear wheels so that I circumvented an overloaded bicycle in time.

"Why have you left out your mother-in-law?" I jibed at the cyclist, who had his entire family tree balanced precariously in every available crevice of the cycle.

He spat vociferously in my direction; the saliva glob graced his handlebar on which was also perched a toddler looking happily up at the sky expecting early monsoons.

"And don't hunch all over the steering wheel, clutching it hard like the car wants to go elsewhere," came my daughter's advice.

I was glad when we were finally home and I could switch off the FM woman's post-coital banter, unload groceries and begin to examine the foodstuff. It looked like we could feed a starving army, but actually this would disappear in two days. It was all the crinkly, coloured plastic wraps, taking up space and making us pay more. Everything pinched me now, now that I was alone and unarmed…. Okay, okay, things are not so bad, but it is worth it to go "poor me" once in a while just to see if my tear-glands worked.

"Let's open the curtains," I called out cheerfully to banish some of the emptiness of the house, and giggled as well, there are no curtains yet; I hadn't got around to the smaller things. There's something eerie about old houses on the verge of being pulled down, a mélange of dust-motes and leftover moods in legacy from previous tenants.

For a moment I was tempted to squeeze back into the car and drive about aimlessly. With hands on the wheel I feel in control, I'm actually going somewhere, there's background music and if you're sick, there's always the window. Ah, well. I could have it worse. I could be without my kids who hate me pathologically, who I love pathologically. You see, I multiplied with great difficulty. Some women are born fertile; they just have to look at a man to miss a period, but my ovum had been most reluctant to go public.

"Your hair," suddenly announced Kuttoose, "makes you look like a man."

I had chopped it all off, which sounds a bit grand, like I had this long silky mane of irresistible hair and sold it to mermaids for down payment on an underwater castle. It was either look like a man or go bald.

I am tired. Tonight I will unhook the phone, a newborn MTNL connection I received with maternal pride, but what the hell, blank calls at midnight were no lullaby. About the doorbell there was nothing I could do, except play ball by not reacting. Whoever heckled me wanted me heckled, so I kept things to myself, not confiding in that unhygienic woman who came two hours every day to do my chores. Actually she does get things done, even though it interrupts her routine staring into space and scratching unmentionables. I don't want it to get about. How sorry it sounds; a woman living alone with a child, doorbell pealing all night. No, the idea was to look tough, manly as K said, like I'd eat my own kids if no one was watching.

I put the cottage cheese into the pan, satisfied with the smell of burnt onions wafting across my kitchen. I love it when things go wrong, when table legs wobble and vendors act wonky; it was precisely this penchant for imperfection that set me down this road. For then you know something perfectly sane is going on inside of you. It is hard to explain this certainty, but when you call people over and everything is going like clockwork, you just know you will burst all over the place after they leave. I don't know which comes first though, the perfection or the messy aftermath.

"Puhleeze," drawled my aged daughter, eyeing my manic cooking. "Relax, okay."

Eating disgusts K. Rolling elderly eyeballs, sighing superannuated sighs, she sauntered off into the bedroom. This was a one-bedroom house, though we pretended it wasn't, especially when I shouted, "Go to your room, now!" or when she flounced off in a huff and slammed that door shut.

Next I called my son, who was with my husband in a neat division of labour. My hello was swallowed up by his yawn; poignant boredom being his thing.

"I am fine," he said. "Papa is fine. Everything is fine."

"Tell me what you ate for dinner?"

Whispered confabulations. "I ... er ... we ate out. Something nutritious."

Sure, like *chaat*. "That's nice," I enthused blandly, ever the bower and scraper though salt coats my eye. "What about the cook you mentioned?"

"Didn't work out. Asked too much."

Suddenly I seethed. Out of nowhere sneaked up this scattered sense of outrage, sending the bower and scraper scurrying for cover. "What's he trying to save for at the expense of your life? I haven't asked for anything. I mean, the car is practically dying. Except that, what have I taken? Why isn't he feeding you, that ... that *paragon*?"

"Hysterical," he was muttering.

I breathed deeply and took the sleeping pill and

the tummy pill and the multi-vitamin pill, feeling like a freak, feeling like I'd lose my dinner. Now for some sweet dreams with Prince Valium, who I hoped would press my ctrl.alt.del.

K was already curled around the makeshift pillow I had fashioned out of double-decking car cushions. Hysterical! Why must I be the scaredy-cat, unplugging my phone? Let the creep call and let the heavy breathing begin. Can't wait, in fact.

I positioned the phone next to the cheap alarm clock on the windowsill next to me, having locked the windows – primly covered with an old sari pallu – so that no wanton streetlight dared to spill in through their seams. I wanted hush and I wanted sleep, oh how I wanted sleep.

I was too bushwhacked to even imagine being burgled. Let's face it, what will a burglar burgle in my house? Unless he is one of those lazy ones who works for a syndicate and is paid no matter how paltry the pickings. Why do I even think these things, defend the unknown, grow garbled over trivia and non-existent pilferage? And what idiot will rob after ringing the bell?

Then the doorbell rang. It is my mind playing tricks I thought. But K groaned an obscenity in sleep so the bell must have rung. Too tired even to grumble, I slithered out without disturbing her further.

My son stood at the door.

"You bitch," he addressed me almost conversationally.

His channel-surfing eyes were red-rimmed. A motorbike revved urgently behind him and he stumbled away from the door.

I ran out but he had already straddled the pillion seat. The motorbike snorted and took off like a wailing banshee down the road. There was no sleep after that. Deep inside, I know, he knows who I am. He always has. He knows I am no bitch, but his mother, who is sometimes a bitch, but never to him.

I prepared to spend the rest of the night watching K's face, relaxed into her approximate age on the pillow.

As I tossed and turned, my ex-husband called. So and so hospital, he ordered, and I dragged my ass pronto. I knew why I had been called when the hospital staff ceremoniously prepared me for taking blood. My son needs blood and unfortunately my husband's group does not match.

I had not been summoned because I am his mother. I had not been summoned for providing solace to the man I once married. Just for a beaker of blood. Well.

"If it wasn't a rare group and it wasn't so late…." my former husband let his voice trail off.

"How bad is he hurt?"

"I … don't know."

This alarmed me. This man has been many things to me but he has never been kind.

"The other guy is a goner."

"The one who drove like a lunatic?" At his

questioning eye, I absently recounted our son's midnight visit to me.

"You see," he spluttered, immediately reassembling into the man I remember. "You see now what you have done to him. You have gone and killed him."

He has office to attend and my daughter has school, so my ex-husband and I exchange offspring duties. K goes off with him. They have other lives to which they return while I stay on and wait for my son to open his eyes.

The hospital canteen has a menu put up on the wall but everything tastes of Dettol, even the potable water. My son cannot eat as yet, he is on a drip with an intravenous supply of liquid glucose, which they replace bottle after bottle and I worry that his taste buds will die this way.

A month into his coma and the spirit has begun to flag though I am loath to admit it being his mother and therefore the unofficial spokesperson for his soul.

My prayers have changed texture. I no longer ask God that my son do an MBA or that he keep down an MNC job or uncork me a fizzy daughter-in-law.

I just want him up and about. Not be this ... vegetable. I want him to tell me what a lousy mom I am. How Sandeep's mother does this, does that. That was when he was in kindergarten and I have hated the mothers of every Sandeep in the world since then.

Please God, let him wake up and call me names. Seeing him lying there day after day, his hand on the sheet where I lay it last, it sticks the food in my throat. Please God, I prayed, no longer embarrassed to say it aloud, just let him open his eyes.

I doze off and on. In the midst of crayoned dreams I automatically throw a glance at my son and notice that his eyes, they are open! I know what to do, of course. I am supposed to ring the emergency bell, inform the nurses, who in turn will call the doctors. But I do no such thing.

I go closer to my son and look deep into those eyes. They are open without a blink and they move as I move. My tongue is thick with sleep and spit so I don't even try to speak but my eyes are shining I know and I watch his eyes in return, to recognise, to question, to shine back at me.

He watches me with a new wariness, one I have not seen before. There is an unnerving blankness in his eyes. He has no idea who I am, I read there. There is no rancour in there for abandoning him and there is no joy at seeing me again.

I am no one to him right this moment; his eyes don't call me mom, his eyes don't call me bitch. They hold none of the pleasant wonder I remember from the time he smelt milk on me for the first time in the delivery room of this same hospital fifteen years ago.

There is nothing in his eyes now except a growing and terrifying nothingness.

"He doesn't know...." My voice breaks and the night nurse flashing a torch into his eyes turns to me impatiently.

The room is growing unmanageably large, I want to say, but I am scared.

"...Me."

GREEN EARRINGS

I cruised the infamous street back and forth in the luminous dryness of a chocolate box sunset. Last time it had taken me over an hour but tonight there was a made-over tribal bimbo wandering mincingly, her awkward gait signifying one too many customers. She was what my wife would have dismissed as HMT – the Hindi-medium type.

Not that I chose indiscriminately. It was the green of the two make-believe emeralds gored into the cubby-holes of her earlobes that decided me, the incandescent green loops in those lacerations; a pair of cheap earrings if you please.

Inside the car she tossed out the corn on the cob she had been nibbling at and turned pure hostess, permanently on smile, well versed with today's specials.

She had on a short batik wrap-around skirt that she kept pulling down convulsively. A healed scar graced one bare knee, cataloguing the urchin touch. I usually avoid storing up personal details for fear of unwanted reminiscence except, of course, the green. The green is a must, it is all I look for, see, latch on to....

A glint on the sunshiny surface of a collected pool or the shimmer of trashy jewellery, fronds of fungi stationed on watery stillness refracting needle-sharp shards of light in crystalline peaks of contaminated droplets, incandescently fresh as the crunchy grass under-foot. A greener-than-green green.

I shrugged away her customary caress, the fingers trailing like clammy spider webs, and stonewalled forays into small talk with ill-timed brakes, pauses and incoherent mutterings. A sideways glance confirmed her nerviness, not full-blown, just a tinge, enough to make her lapse into blessed silence.

Once we reached the bungalow, she breathed deep under the low-slung stars, "Ooh!"

Her awe burgeoned as she witnessed more of the gloating architectural ambience. Its painstaking cobble-stoned driveway, the stubble of radiant shrubs sprayed with dew, beauty-parloured lawns, satin-finish walls in creamy shades of peach, the egoistic hue and cry in its every designer brick and marbled slab, all done up to dazzle.

No credit to me; the exteriors came with the gift, the house was my aristocratic father-in-law's way of saying "Match this!" on my engagement day, and the interiors completely consumed his mint-eyed daughter. She got it done professionally and with maximum interference and expenditure before we moved in, our wedding delayed until they got the house decorated, burnished just so and the icing iced to their puritanical Kashmiri Pundit perfection.

I glanced at the aesthetic compost heap at the bottom of the garden as I always do – there is no ophthalmologic apparatus there, but eerily enough I feel ogled – before turning into home.

Inside, the whore bowed to a sliced flower snuggling amidst much unrelated foliage in a gigantic crystal vase, the extinct scent going to her head judging by the fuss she made. I plucked a leaf and buried my nose in its green bulging veins. Closer, until my iris vibrated with it. Closer. A blink and the chlorophyll cordoned off in my eye.

Barely had we entered the self-conscious foyer, she wrapped herself around me, to fast-forward whatever lay ahead. "Darrling," she Englished in a rush, having consigned me to the upper classes and worthy of her best.

I extricated myself from the skinny arms, leading her wordlessly to the bedroom for our commercial transaction. And then it was done and she was gone.

The door shut, I shivered in the gummy coolness.

Undressing completely now I turned to the shower. As the water sluiced down me in the butter-hued bathroom, I watched the cupboard against which I had demonstrated my prowess.

"Perform," my wife used to exhort, the moon alight in each greenish pupil mirroring a devil-tailed mockery. "Do it like a man." Until I came home one day, into this showpiece home of hers, and saw her writhing in bed, our bed, under.... I had never seen those two men before in my life whereas she ... she never saw them again.

I looked up to where she stared from, her severed head cleverly hidden in a bulky silk-lined paper-bag with two slits cut for sight, and raised my water-slicked eyebrows, quizzing her about my latest performance.

KISS AND TELL

"You what?"

Incredulously she dropped the light bag she carried on to the carpeted hotel floor.

"You heard me," he said calmly, heaving the heavier suitcase on to a rack above the doorway. "I called him up and said take her out to dinner, she is crazy about you."

"You are joking," her voice lilted with fake amusement.

He did not reply. Instead he walked over to the only table provided in the room on which sat a telly and sundry practical objects like the newspaper, tea things etc and plugged the kettle on. Then he picked up the Styrofoam cups and placed them neatly on the plastic tray, dropping the teabags into them like two suicidal kites.

"Leave that," she muttered, but she knew he'd go ahead and make tea before looking at her face, a face he hadn't seen for an entire year. She walked over to the window and looked desultorily below, at women scurrying about with onward bosoms – no rest for the breast – and their low-waist, semi-gynaecological pants. Ever since hers bungee-jumped, she took a dim view of breasts per se.

"Here," he handed her a cup, warning, "it is hot."

For a moment she was tempted to make a sarcastic remark, but bit it back. It was the jetlag, she decided, you can't travel non-stop for hours and be bright and chatty at the end of it.

"Tell me about the journey," he invited.

Looking up she smiled, reminding herself that this was all about "making an effort" like her mother said.

"It's been so long."

He looked faintly surprised, as if she was meandering into intimacy too early. He had, she knew, an internal clock that he followed in personal relationships. He could compartmentalize his hours, tastes, affection, and oh how she had hated being in one of those compartments! But a year apart had helped her to gloss over; of course, her mother could peep into that part of her heart she couldn't.

"I know you," her mother had declared, dangling her ridiculously short legs over the sofa's edge. "Always eyeing others' plates."

Some mothers liked to think their daughters eternal

virgins, some feared them hopeless sluts. Her own mother fell into the latter category. She remembered when she was twelve and had opened the door to someone totally forgettable, postman perhaps, and mother had come panting out of the toilet, flush still flushing, to dart suspicious looks at the door as if she expected it to be splattered with fresh semen.

"You didn't really do that, did you?" she asked him now, swallowing tea with difficulty.

"See," he said, "I want you to get it out of your system. Ever since you told me about your infatuation, I've been uncomfortable."

His discomfort was nothing compared to hers. She had been light-headed with starvation that day, having had no time to gulp down breakfast or lunch since it had been a busy time at the bank with everyone in the world wanting to draw out or stack up money. Saturdays were half-days anyway, so lunch was always a late one at home, but that day she had gone shoe-shopping in Karol Bagh and then the impromptu rains diverted every auto-rickshaw militantly away so that she trudged down the deep-throated road on foot. It was with disappointment that she had confronted their guest.

"I have bullied him into staying for dinner," her husband called out gaily while she wrung out her dupatta in relative privacy.

What irked her an hour later was that they went on like she was non-existent. She just sat there guzzling the brandy her husband had insisted would make her feel better and felt increasingly bonsai. No wonder then by the time they went to bed she was restless and talkative. And so it was that she told him about her undying passion for the bank manager.

Then he had sat up blinking. "You mean that man who came here to pick you up on the transport strike day?"

She had happily agreed with a hiccup. "Yes, him. You are right. All the women love him, mind you, but I really love him, really. No one loves him like that in the office. I can love him till I die. Oh yes, I can. I love him."

At least that's what he quoted to her the next morning, unfortunately a Sunday when she was trapped by his side with nowhere to go, nothing to do. She had slept late and long, waking up to a hangover and his bad humor.

"You've been emotionally unfaithful to me and that is worse than … than if you had just slept with him one night. I can understand lust, but not sustained adoration. It is downright adultery!"

She was dimly aware that if she had confessed to exchanging bodily fluids instead of yearning looks, he would have freaked XXL size; hers had been a very politically correct infidelity. By night despite her breathless protestations about girlish fantasies he had shifted bedrooms, and war was officially declared.

At first she tried to joke it off. She told all her

close colleagues, the ones who clicked open their lunch-boxes around her, carefully withholding the identity of the object of her affection.

"It is just a crush, yaar," she laughed. "Nothing."

"But not to husbands," the others mourned for her, biting into pickles or puris or whatever their maids or mothers-in-law had stuffed into their lunch-boxes. "You can do whatever with whomever, but never tell."

She had gasped, unable to imagine these sedate women go home with soiled lunch boxes and knickers.

In the history of their marriage it had always been him who made the first move. Still, one brave night she sought him out and then shivered foolishly in her camisole when he had turned away.

"I am going abroad," he told her two weeks later. He had been trying to secure admission for visual arts in California for some time now, so she really did not need to hang low her jaw in surprise but she thought his travel plan totally out of context. On the eve of his departure she had been sobbing into her pillow when he tapped her on a shoulder.

She crumbled at that touch instantaneously, piteously whimpering for additional contact, and he had been magnanimous in ceasefire, she had to give him that. The whole night she had talked garbled and feverish of her love for him, of her bone-deep awareness of marital duties right up to marrow etc and he had nodded seriously, signing her bail papers.

A year later, burning up with the desire to meet him, she had begged and pleaded at the bank for a junket to US and one lucky day followed her boss to California for software training.

"He's in Room 14," her husband informed her with the preciseness of a concierge. He checked his watch. "You have fifteen minutes to get ready."

She realized he read her hormones, left to right, the same as her mother and hoped to wring out the slut in her in one masterly stroke.

Resolutely she got up and unzipped her bag. He watched her, baffled by this abrupt acquiescence, as she came out of the bath and struggled into the tight tunic-dress she had picked up from Cottage Emporium, hoping to lose weight on the flight.

She threw him a coquettish smile, "Room 14 you said."

She was calling his bluff; anytime now he'd break down and hug her. But he didn't.

Her boss opened the door. "What happened?" he asked and instantly she knew she had been tricked, it had been a trap. There had been no phone call to this man, there was no dinner planned, just a mad spouse at one end and she at the other.

"Can I come in?" she asked.

"Of course," he moved aside, still watching her with some trepidation.

"He has gone to sleep and I am ... you know jetlag. So I just wondered if you'd mind eating with me."

He turned around and preceded her into a room larger than hers, his bald patch winking at her.

As the evening wore on, they discovered a mutual liking for old Hindi songs, trashy films and summery weather, in themselves not electrifying enough to warrant a mention, but the bonhomie was welcome. It was with regret that she stood up.

"That was nice," she said awkwardly at the doorway.

"Yes," he agreed soberly, not averse to undercurrents inherent in feminine company at such late hour.

They watched each other and swooped in slow motion, stopping mid-way, her lips an inch under his nose, his Santa stomach upon her galloping heart.

"Th ... thank you," she mumbled, inhaling the coleslaw on his breath, her eyeballs refracting the overhead light. "I'll leave now."

"Agreed," he agreed.

A footstep in the corridor; she knew who it was.

"Goodnight," she said, leaning away.

He looked beyond her, at her husband's clothes, the flowers in his hands, his anxious expression, and closed the door.

She retraced her steps to the lift, maddeningly silent.

"Well?" he asked back in the room.

She smiled, flopping down on the crisp-sheeted bed in her evening clothes, knowing it irritated the hell out of him.

"So...?"

She shut her eyes as if to arrest a sweet dream, heard

him aim the roses at the waste-bin, where they fell with a soft swish.

"I missed you," he said to her back.

Two Legends in One

Mrs Demon was throwing a fit. "I am not sick. I do not have a disease. I am only pregnant."

"Right, dear," soothed Mr Demon, eyes on the newspaper. Suddenly he began to laugh. "These demons I tell you...." Catching his wife's eye he assumed his most caring greeting-card expression. "I know, I know, it seems forever. But only one more month, darling, then it will be over."

"Fat lot you know." Mrs Demon paused to wipe the vomit off her chin. Everyone was having fun, rushing here and there for picnics and parties. The glorious weather wouldn't last, the sales wouldn't go on, the gaiety in the air was not going to pause for her! Here she was, with Little Demon on the way, bulkier and bulgier than their monthly grocery bag. Damned if she was going to look ecstatic to boot. She groaned to illustrate her last thought.

"Okay, okay," her husband got up hurriedly and began to clumsily rub her back with his big, hairy hand. Keeping demonesses barefoot and pregnant took more out of him than he could afford to give!

Mrs Demon crumpled some paper in her hand.

"What's that, dear?" he asked, knowing a cue when he heard one.

"Nothing."

He rubbed her back.

"It's nothing."

He continued to rub her back. Big, hairy hand going up and down, up and down.

"I mean, it is the invitation to the Big Bash."

The Big Bash, an annual event in Demon-land, was where all demons met and frolicked and caught up with each other and generally let down their matted hair. It was like a pub, a disc, a garden, a park, all at once.

She sighed nostalgically. That was where they had met in the first place and also the spot where she could rejoin her family members.

Mr Demon knew what he had to do, had to say. "I was thinking, dear...."

Mrs Demon went very still for she knew what was coming.

"I was thinking that maybe I could ... temporarily

take on your pregnancy for the weekend while you go there and enjoy your time-out."

"I'll come back on Sunday night," she promised eagerly, having thought of nothing but this potential offer for a long while. "I promise. Just let me go without … this."

At midnight, Mr and Mrs Demon heaved stomachs at each other. Bumped to belly, they chanted invocations, wrenching thunder and lightning from the calm sky. The noise and fury caused them to close their eyes and when they opened them, Mr Demon was with child and Mrs Demon had her old waistline, which was large and blubbery, back.

She did a little jig, making incoherent sounds, and the house began to wobble a bit.

"Careful, dear." Mr Demon said, trying to stem the sudden nausea.

But she had zoomed up the staircase to pack her overnight case. When she came down, he was still bent over, retching.

"I'll call you," she said, almost airborne with joy. "Shall stay with my niece." And she skipped off, with nary a backward glance, not heeding the wobble of their residential foundation or of her husband's chin.

Now the niece wasn't what you'd call nice. She was, if you asked Mr Demon, a nasty piece of work. One of those feminist types and he had a dark foreboding of things to come. Fortunately the pregnancy was full-time and almost full-term, so he was spared too much brooding, what with visits to doctors, sudden culinary cravings, mood swings, keeping down food and flatulence.

On Sunday morning he sat up in his bed and screamed. He couldn't locate his feet! It took him a while to realize that his vision was obstructed, that he could no longer see his feet owing to a bloated tummy.

There they were, his feet, he thought with relief and thrust them into furry slippers. Then he jogged to the bathroom as he wanted to barf and ease bladder simultaneously.

He emerged weakly without brushing his teeth to consume some emergency caffeine. Mrs Demon had expressly stayed off coffee and he himself had piously told her of the harm it could do to the fetus, but now he found that cola, caffeine and nicotine made this never-ending weekend more bearable.

Then he took himself off to office where he was keener to discuss his condition than to get any work done. When he came home there was a telegram waiting for him. "Staying back," it said, that's all. Just two words:

1. Staying.
2. Back.

Presumably it came from his partying wife. But bleary-eyed he really couldn't bring himself to begin cursing, though cursing was what he had majored in in college.

What did she mean? Perhaps a longer vacation. But

the due date loomed large. And ... at that point bile made an appearance at the backdoor of his throat, so he had to press the pause button again. Then he had to wipe the puke off the floor, so he had to pause again. At the back of his mind was the horrific thought; maybe she planned this. That damned niece of hers!

When he could sit up, he rang her up, but the cell-phone intoned, "Your number is being routed."

He called the niece in the absence of an alternative.

"Yes?" she said, knowing full well who he was and what he felt.

"Is she there?"

"Oh. Haven't you heard? She has moved in with a really dishy demon from uptown."

Mr Demon moaned. He had to. His water just broke.

In his next birth Mr Demon came down in human form, as a Hindu Brahmin in Hyderabad to be precise. As long as he could, he retained his bachelor status, which wasn't too difficult as he was running a guru-kul where his students stayed with him and the logistics and administrative headaches sufficed to busy him. But on his fortieth birthday he chanced upon a calendar from a local brewery and the semi-clad damsels on it, page after page, month after month. The hind limbs of the November nymphet and the two-mammary army of the May model caused excess saliva in his mouth, sweat in his palm and a mutiny in his own pants.

He told his dhobi, the dhobi told his wife and the wife contacted the unofficial marriage bureau. Now there were too many choices before the good Brahmin. His virtuous past and affluent present combined to bring him the best in matrimonial pickings.

He skipped past innocent divorcees, studious singletons and menstruating widows to settle for a beauty from a poverty-stricken family. The marriage was duly solemnized and the sixteen-year-old bride stepped over his threshold one damp rainy noon amidst much tuneless flute-playing.

He was her husband and teacher, too, as academics were his world. He taught her about virtue and devotion to husband and piety. She seemed an apt student, for just when he dismissed his gurukul, not wanting adolescent boys with their horny eyes lurking amidst the mangroves, she confined herself to the basement. Here she let him exercise his conjugal rights only in the dark, without even the flame of candlelight.

"I do not want you, my husband but a man nonetheless, to witness me," she demurred.

And he marvelled at her feminine modesty. When she conceived, she said, "If it is a girl-child, I will look after her myself. But if it is a boy, then I will never set eyes on him. He may be my son but he would be a man."

Though this baffled him somewhat, he could gauge the staunch morality that drove the non-maternal sentiment and duly gave in when a man was born to them.

Thus she stayed, cocooned and shielded from male eyes, virtue personified, morality incarnate and nothing pleased the old Brahmin more than this ardent fidelity of his young wife.

Then the King called all learned men for a National Conference on the Soul and the Brahmin picked up his briefcase with some trepidation.

"You will be all right?" he asked doubtfully. He was loath to send her back to her father's place, where strange men with their perverted vision may come ogling.

"I shall not stir from this basement," she vouched.

The conference took just two days and though the Brahmins were asked to stay back for the official dinner, this anxious Brahmin embarked on his return journey almost immediately, thinking what a pleasant surprise it would be for his wife to see him back thus a day early.

It was late evening when he reached home, but what was this, his gate was unlatched! And there were two fat candles dripping wax merrily in the living room. On the rug lay his wife, the candlelight bright on her bareness, with the man who shimmied up trees and plucked coconuts for a living.

He ran in, sure she was being violated in the most

unimaginable way. Their eyes met then. He hovered uncertainly at the doorway when she put up a palm, while her lover panted away. When he was done, he turned around and upon sighting the Brahmin uttered a shriek, gathered his clothes and fled, all in one smooth move no doubt made easier by the nature of his profession.

She sat up languorously, the satisfied smirk playing on her reddened lips not lost on him.

"The light?" he stammered, for he had not *seen* her in a long while.

"Anything to hide your wrinkly lust."

"Son?" What reason she had to hate an offspring so?

"Yours," she spat. "It was *yours*."

In his next birth, not surprisingly, he switched genders and bothered some man instead.

THE TIARA

Sex? Hmmm, life goes on, thanks for asking. Nine years of marriage does take away the edge, you know. But no complaints, nothing kinky on the anvil, infidelity nil. Unless you count my dreams. Great gusts of lust sweep me in my sleep, combing through and through; though at dawn I can recall neither dream nor its inhabitants, the emotion still juddered through me, ripping brutally my monogamous mask. The sight of Akshara sleeping by my side, fist on pillow, is sobering. And, well, you know dreams, how they come and go.

With Aksha it was the name that had arrested, much like my wife's, a name I was so used to. The alliteration held my attention as Akshara plumped up the cushion on her knee. "Nanu's niece."

Nanu's niece was nicely draped in layers of muslin, yards and yards of dupatta fluttering down, glass bangles clinking, sweet fragrance floating up as she waved a languid hand; so stereotypically feminine like a B-grade Hindi film heroine unlike my wife in her sensible shorts and summery top.

Amused, I waved back.

Aksha and Akshara struck up a fierce friendship; both were at a loose end what with one trying to decide on a degree and the other, my ovulating half, trying for a baby.

"She is so sweet," my wife said and just when I began to imagine a superior variety of sugar, I was told about Aksha's susceptible stomach.

Eventually she joined a computer course not far from here and my wife conceived. Through these two momentous events I was kept continuously and breathlessly posted on Aksha's delicate stomach so that her digestion became a regular conversation topic at our house. All she wanted, allegedly, was silky-smooth – no, not hair or skin – bowels.

Holi fell on the fourth month; the baby was kicking hard and exhausting Akshara. Her friend was here, in and out, minding our kitchen, defrosting the fridge or generally keeping the domestic help in line. On Holi, Akshara woke up early. Since the nausea had abated somewhat she was determined to celebrate the festival like she always did. To this end the previous night the two buddies had positioned drums on the terrace, bought colour globules guaranteed to turn you more hopelessly purple or pink with each wash, and topped this with a million water balloons.

We had had pani-puris for dinner in deference to Akshara's tastebuds, and when tamarind juice trickled down Aksha's chin, Akshara handed me a napkin and Aksha thrust her chin at me for wiping like a little girl.

I watched the preparations lazily, my mind more on the crib Akshara had pointed out in Paharganj. I was determined to make it myself though she was inclined to roll eyes and call me "Carpenter-ji" mockingly. Scrounging around for some wooden planks in the garage downstairs later in the day, I saw Aksha slyly shoot up the stairs, the line of her spine radiating mischief. Picking the planks I needed, I made my way up the stairs. The front door was open. Aksha, stalking Akshara, turned to me with a giggle.

A fluorescent orange moustache glowed under her nose and it was obvious she thirsted for revenge. Both women faced each other, bosoms heaving, watching each other like kabaddi adversaries.

Akshara glanced at the door again as if someone had just walked in, tricking. When Aksha turned to look, she ran into her bedroom, fingers flying to bolt the door from inside. In a trice Aksha was on her tail. They pushed the door from both sides energetically and I was tempted to call out to Akshara to take it easy though I knew it wouldn't be welcome since these days she liked to retort she was not a "multiplication table."

Aksha threw open the door victoriously and like Hanuman handing Ram the whole mountain for Laxman's treatment, she emptied her entire stock of powder on a wriggling Akshara who had collapsed weak-kneed backward into bed. It was like a colour bomb had exploded on our bedspread.

My wife held the other's wrists in her hands, stilling those clinky-gossipy bangles, with Aksha poised atop, breasts against each other's, open mouths panting and limbs inter-twined. A camera whirred in my cranium, so sharp were the hues of the moment etched in my mind, my memory. Hormones spelt out diktat; in a split second my dreams were dyed forever.

Now they are predictable, my slumbers and their aftermath. Each time the infant yowls, his wails walk backward into me and them, together somewhere, anywhere, bodies finger-painted, glistening wetly to the gills with warm splashes, the three of us poised at Technicolor precipices of my subconscious' suggestion when I coronate two queens.

PILLOW TALK

"Catch me flying off to anywhere! I mean I'm just back from a backbreaking trip and the idiot wants me gone again. I say no."

She wished he'd park the company car and get out of it before whining. Now there was a slight dent on the bonnet where he punctuated his ire with a reversing bang.

"Don't go if you...."

"You have no opinions of your own," he cut in. "Your job is so easy! Just go along with what the idiot husband says. Safe that way. I mean no boss is going to rip your ass off tomorrow."

"You'd be surprised," she thought, smiling her ice-on-green-chillies smile. "Must we conduct every conversation for our neighbours? Come inside, it's cool in there and we've got *samosas*."

"The greasy things," he muttered, sinking into a sofa, wagging a finger. "Trying to kill me just like him. Only he tries to toss me around the world like a postal parcel and you … why don't you just deep-fry *me* instead?"

He sat right under the ebony carving of a miniature man carrying proportionately miniature firewood. Crucified to the wall twice, once by head, once by ankles for a linear symmetry, the nail between its feet dangled like a fallen penis. Parallel to her husband's wagging finger, she observed.

"Your cholesterol is under control, that's what the doctor said. A little oil now and then can't hurt," she soothed, then altering pitch she called out, "Jamuna."

Jamuna meandered in with much tinkling of bangles and anklets, like a belled cow in a meadow.

"Get Saab chai, less sugar and listen, bring just two samosas," she was instructed, though she duly re-entered with two cups of tea, sugar in a separate bowl and four samosas in a pretty china saucer, not fancying scurrying to and fro while they chewed and changed their minds. Saab ate like a pig.

As the tealeaves worked their magic, he calmed down enough to coherently complain. "He just called me in out of the blue, saying the project in Nainital is stuck at some sensitive level and needs my intervention right away. I mean if I am so indispensable then how come they do not need me here, in my own little cubicle." He began to hiccup, samosa embedded deep in gullet.

"Jamuna, water," she screamed.

Again the tinkling and jingling as water came in two glasses on a tray. As Jamuna bent over and he picked up a glass, the other affectionately rolled into his lap; not Jamuna, but the glass.

"What...."

"I specifically told you one glass of water," she remonstrated.

"You didn't," Jamuna stuck to her guns, shaking the empty tray like a housewife at a Tupperware party. "You just yelled for water."

"Where do you get these retards?" he hollered, plucking at his fly.

Now if only the glass had tilted at his skull! "You were saying?" she prompted aloud when Jamuna had cut a pastoral exit.

He looked at her blankly before recouping to declare, "I am not a child, to be told sit here, go there. No one can tell me what to do."

No, that's a privilege only his mother has. "Don't tell me you are not going!"

"I am not," he retorted triumphantly, a double-whammy of refuting her and his boss at one go.

"But your bags are packed!"

"How come?"

"They ... they have not been unpacked since you came back yesterday. Besides, what will you say?"

"Anything," he shrugged, not being partial to details, yawning and stretching his arms languorously, almost giving the Firewood Man on the wall a hand-job. "My car broke down I can say…." he broke off as the phone began to trill. "Don't pick it up. Must be him, to check whether I have jumped as high as he said. Tell him I left, no, wait, tell him … first pick it up you idiot."

She picked it up, cooing a peacenik "hello" into it. "No, no, wrong number," she said, putting the receiver down. She got up with a delicate cough, heading for the stairway.

"Where are you going?" he asked plaintively.

"To the loo."

But she had barely reached upstairs and picked up her mobile, when he was breathing down her neck. "The AC is on here and down? Go switch off the one down."

She leant down the railing. "Jamuna, AC bandh kar do."

"Yeah, and let our electric connections go to the dogs." He shook his head.

"Yes, I have gone to school, both primary and high," she said automatically because at this point it was customary for him to scratch his head and ask, "Have you never gone to school?"

He proceeded to enter the bathroom, bathe and change into pyjamas.

"I am going to sleep," he declared, walking out with a multi-coloured towel wrapped around his head, which he said prevented hair-loss. As he prepared to lie down, in a rare show of interest, he enquired, "What will you do?"

"TV," she said and he scrunched up his face as if she should invent a cure for AIDS in her spare time.

But TV was her only weapon when it came to killing time, second by second, hour by hour, day by day. That and the telephone, but that was out, for this man would never sleep, only eavesdrop. And his tongue she feared. Of all the languages he knew, he was the most fluent in sarcasm.

The low volume of the TV as the heroine rambled on about unwed motherhood was soporific enough to make her jump when he appeared in the doorway, the towel on his head disorienting her further, whispering hoarsely, "He is here."

"Who?" she asked, sure he meant to say "she." Persecuted by maternal nightmares, he often dreamt of his mother chasing him naked with a sword down his old school.

"He. That man. My boss. The idiot."

"Oh, him."

"Switch off all the lights. The bastard is here to check on me. You ... don't move. Keep sitting here, watching TV. Tell Jamuna, we are sleeping. I mean, tell her to say I am not here and that you are sleeping."

She went to the railing again. "Jamuna...."

Jamuna, who drew the line at tinkling up the stairs at odd hours, shouted right back, "*Haan-ji.*"

"Tell her, tell her," he muttered feverishly.

"Tell the saab I am sleeping."

"I am not coming all the way up to tell saab you are sleeping. You know about my gout...."

"The saab who is coming," she notified even as the doorbell began to peal. "Tell him our saab is not here and that I am sleeping."

Jamuna made no response, but could be heard opening the door.

They turned the TV off and he crouched on his fours near her knees, adjusting his terry turban; footsteps came up the stairs and they registered the absence of anklets.

"What the...." He managed to dive behind the bookshelf just in time to watch his boss enter with a "hi" quite at variance with his customary bark.

His wife, who was frantically finger-combing her hair, twittered, "It was you. It is you. I mean you."

"Yes, me," he affirmed, "You look lovely."

"No, I just woke up, haven't done anything...."

"Gorgeous," he reiterated in a booming voice the husband behind the bookshelf recognized, that brooked no opposition, that meant I am boss.

"Yes," she agreed meekly.

He leaned forward, lips stabbing air.

She tried to gesture at the bookshelf but he got it all wrong. "Okay I will stand here," he said, standing by the bookshelf, eyes shut, "and you can come and kiss me instead."

She looked at him and then at the pair of open

eyes between two over-priced encyclopaedias bought to embellish the shelf.

"Let her let him kiss her, let her let him kiss her," her husband was chanting silently into the encyclopaedias, repeatedly swishing his eyeballs to the left, directing her. She obeyed him as if he had picked up the TV remote and directed it at her, though the slurpy quality of the kiss flustered him. No need to put your heart, soul and saliva into what was just a kiss-ass kiss.

There was the sound of ripping and her buttons flew this way and that.

"I sent the idiot to Nainital," the boss said, "disposing of him is getting tougher and tougher by the day. Today I thought he'd outright refuse."

She gestured urgently to the shelf. He shook his head indulgently. "Taking off those books would take time. Let's do it on the floor today."

She had the good sense to lean over and shove the twin encyclopaedias against each other, thus blocking her husband's range of vision but activating mud molecules on the books dusted by Jamuna with a wholly spiritual hand. The bookshelf sneezed violently.

"My husband," she whispered as her lover stared at the bookshelf. "Your boss," she said in a louder voice. And her husband crept out, still on his fours, the towel fanning out like a multi-coloured wig.

"You!" said the boss when he had straightened. "This is Nainital?"

"No, sir. I mean, this is almost my bedroom, sir."

"I came by to see … if your wife needed anything."

"I can see that, sir."

"And I was just leaving, anyway."

"And I was just leaving for Nainital, sir."

"I think let it be, eh? I got a phone call," he added vaguely. "Still, you should let me know such things. Can't just decide off your head not to go."

"I was trying your phone all afternoon…." then turning to his wife, he ordered, "Button up. Haven't seen so much breast since I was weaned."

As if he ever was weaned, she thought, struggling to hold the flapping ends of her blouse together.

"That's all, just came by to see she is fine. Shall be off now," boss mumbled in his office voice, moving to the door.

"Saab," Jamuna's bovine bells had gone unheard in the formality of farewells. She held a tray with tea and samosas, angling for her usual tip. "Special for you."

BY A STAFF REPORTER

"Vaale-kum salaam," Gafoorbhai responded to a passerby, one hand skimming his hennaed forelocks, the other firmly around his grandson, Irshad.

It was two years since Gafoorbhai set eyes on Irshad's father, an Armyman posted in Leh, but pride in son's career overrode any personal pining. Also, there was a grandson to keep him company!

Hand in hand, he kept up with the skipping three-year-old. At the sweets shop, the little boy gaped at the bright bottles.

"Tell me what you want," Gafoorbhai cajoled. All day he tried to trick the little boy into speech, but Irshad steadfastly maintained muteness, getting by with an "unnn-unnn" and pointing finger.

"This one?" asked Gafoorbhai, cunningly opening a jar of pickles.

The boy shook his head, pointing at a bottle filled with syrupy pink balls.

"Will wait for his father to come on leave and then he'll say Abba. Children are clever," the shopkeeper guffawed.

Gafoorbhai pretended not to hear, counting out requisite change. It was common knowledge that he wanted his grandson's first word to be "Baba."

"Walk faster," he bade Irshad. They had to hurry to catch the safari in time. The nearby Gir forests had opened up for the summer and March was the best month to sit in their open-roofed jeep and explore the jungle at a bargain fee; neither sultry, nor cool.

At the entrance, he bought one full ticket and one half, and wiping the boy's pink drool, ventured in.

In the jeep, Gafoorbhai scooted over to the edge, letting a sweaty crowd scramble over his bare feet as they filled up the interiors. Even though Irshad sat on his lap, he knew the child would miss most of the scenery if they scooted deep into the jeep's gullet.

The dusty vehicle filled up more than it could carry and an altercation ensued over the number of travellers. Finally, their guide clambered over and shut the grilled door with a clang. "*Chalo*," he bade and the geriatric jeep sputtered into life.

The party soon began to enjoy itself as now a peacock, now a bear played peek-a-boo. The natural habitat here had been painstakingly retained, the flora gleaming an incandescent green in the early noon sun like scattered emeralds. As for fauna, the old man kept an alert lookout; he did not want Irshad to miss anything. The grass was crunching audibly under the jeep's wheels when he spied a tiger peeping from behind a large fir tree.

"Look, Irshad, a tiger."

A shudder of excitement ran through the tourists. Cameras began to whirr as the tiger trailed the jeep, indolently licking a paw.

Irshad clung to his grandfather, whimpering.

"What, you are scared! And your father gone to fight the war." The old man bounced the boy away from his knee. The boy grabbed tight only to be swung high by his grandfather, then out of the jeep's grilled bars.

"Be brave," Gafoorbhai exhorted, raising a shoulder to wipe facial perspiration.

The tiger, in one smooth leap, caught the boy's dangling foot by its jaw. Gafoorbhai frantically pulled but in one bloodied tug of war, the screaming boy arched out of his grasp and was rendered prey.

"They should keep a gun, these guards," the cameraman muttered, adjusting his viewfinder.

The news-anchor swiped a pair of zero-power glasses along her dupatta's edge. "You can't wave red meat at tigers during their feeding time. That will be our angle." She spoke into the mike, "Testing-testing. How did you feel when the animal attacked your grandson? Sound okay?"

Gafoorbhai stared down glassily, head in both hands, unable to rid himself of Irshad's last cry.

He called me Baba, he was thinking, *he called me Baba*.

SPIDER LILIES

Though the fiscal part was not discussed threadbare, it was understood that she wouldn't demur at any miscellaneous domestic detour thrown her way, and Mrs Chatterjee presently had to admit that this maid was a real find. Mrs Chatterjee's mother had made an art form out of picking and training adolescent girls as domestic help and volubly despaired of her elder daughter ever following in her footsteps. But management genes eventually meandered to the rim and Mrs Chatterjee finally found herself taking charge of one entire employee.

Mutely and deferentially, Munnibai would do as told and even untold. For instance, no one actually bade her to harum-scarum retrieve clothes flapping on the line outside if it got dark and cloudy but there she'd be gathering up in the nick of time, a millisecond prior to downpour. The previous maid only muttered sinisterly when the sun played hide and seek; pure gold at punctuality, but when it came to pleasantries, conditions applied.

You could safely ask Munnibai if it was going to rain; she would never retort, "Am I the weather bureau?" Breathing agitatedly via three nostrils – there was a big hole where a nose-pin had once resided like a pre-Raj ruby in the Taj Mahal – she'd just dash outdoors with palms up, testing the air for raindrops.

All in all, as Mrs Chatterjee summarized repeatedly to her husband while he sleepily spooned in his microwaved dinner late at night, "A real find."

And he was happy for her, for when she was unhappy he was rendered a wreck. He had married "higher" and lived in constant fear of her father cutting them off his will or popping it before he got around to the will at all. To that end he and his co-brother-in-law smiled grimly through domestic spats and public humiliations in perfect synchronization. They had married the two beefy sisters with their square jaws and fleshy nostrils while fully conscious, and accepted manfully any attendant anomalies. As far as Mr Chatterjee was concerned, Munnibai could dance naked on the table while dusting it if it kept Mrs Chatterjee in good cheer.

There was only one drawback to settling Munnibai

into the tiny servant-quarters attached to the house: her husband's acute alcoholism. He worked at a still and, going by the reek the first and only time she chanced upon him, Mrs Chatterjee presumed he routinely fell into the vat while stirring. Marinated as he was in the juices of his job, the smell wasn't what she objected to. It was his nocturnal monologues harking back to Munnibai's avatar as his elder sister-in-law once upon a time and his monotonous qualms over her feasible infidelity.

The country-made liquor aerated this usually meek man into pumping up the vernacular volume and raining blows on his wife. It imbued Munnibai with an eternal sadness, like she had been shot in the eye, and caused an odd conflict in the Chatterjee household.

While Mrs Chatterjee routinely applied poultice and philosophy to the injured, Mr Chatterjee was of the opinion that familial matters were best left alone. He was not even prepared to take the drunkard verbally to task.

"Drink's his only relief. Poor man, we should not grudge him his lone recreation."

"But Chatto, his wife, her mother…?"

An envious gleam entered her husband's eye. "Like I said, poor man."

However, she could not just stand by and watch her best maid be butchered slowly and steadily like halal meat. Especially since the children and the old woman would activate a strong wailing system to ward off their turn and set the whole neighborhood cacophonically agog, like a car alarm going off indefinitely and irritatingly bang in the dead of night.

"Hit him back," she suggested, while handing Munnibai a soft cloth to dry the damp glasses, trying not to wince at the almost live bruise on the latter's brow.

Munnibai shot her a pained look. "Bibiji!"

She was watering the spider lilies outside the house and suggesting in her mild, Munnibaish manner that the flowerpot be transferred into the drawing room where it'd be more decorative when Mrs Chatterjee caught up with her later in the day.

"They bloom only outdoors, in the sun," Mrs Chatterjee was categorical as she was about most things, "Leave them here."

Munnibai instantly stopped tugging at the pot and immersed hands in soft dough next. The rigmaroles began to sizzle and blister in the hot oil and one of the junior Chatterjees who came in yelling, "jalebis," got his hand briskly whacked.

"Fasting again?" Mrs Chatterjee rolled her eyes when the maid refused the broken ends of jalebis. Starving in order to prolong spouse's life was inexplicable to her, whose philosophy was until death doth we part, but always best when other party dies first, no?

She bent conspiratorially, "You know what you can do about that husband of yours? Just run out of the house when he starts to beat you. In fact, the moment he raises his hand, run out screaming."

Munnibai said nothing, but that evening she sprinted out yelling blue murder and Mrs Chatterjee missiled a victorious smile at her husband, who smiled back nervously.

This relay race into the colony's common courtyard by the entire servant clan at the slightest provocation from the paternal head bought peace for an entire month. The alcoholic's attempts to rabble-rouse were stymied in a phased manner thus and he was often spotted searching for kith and kin high and low by Mr Chatterjee, who furtively smoked a Gold Flake in the balcony at midnight after Mrs Chatterjee had safely begun to snore.

When Mrs Chatterjee noticed Munnibai limp one day, she did not allude to it at first for fear of being inundated with melodramatic pleas for pity or paise. Then when Munnibai had finished for the day, was preparing to leave and had been handed over some leftover vegetable concoction that could only lead to further flatulence in the Chatterjee household, she asked, non-committal, "Arthritis?"

In answer Munnibai rolled up the functional saree she wore. Mrs Chatterjee gasped at the piping hot welts, the conflagration of bleeding bruises and raw cuts criss-crossed all over her lower limbs like finely shattered crystal. Encouraged by the genuineness of the gasp, Munnibai shifted her pallu and displayed a matching set on her belly.

"He did this to you? Why didn't you...."

Munnibai decorously rearranged the threadbare folds and turned toward the door. "He strips me naked now, so I don't run out."

"The children?"

"Have to watch."

As Mrs Chatterjee's nerves were of paramount importance, Munnibai was disposed of with sincere regret and the last I heard hunt was on for a suitable replacement.

ANGEL WITH ARMPITS

"Check out cloud number nine," solicits an angel at the zebra crossing, her gossamer gown askew.

Am hopeless with directions, not airborne either. Finding Cloud Nine will take me forever, won't it? Spent two whole minutes locating the airy-fairy "pssst" in the first place since angels don't clap owing to silly mix-up with eunuchs and scarcity of aerial shelves to lay down harps.

"Can the cloud be home-delivered?" I tuck in the gray running out behind my ears, pout a couple of cracked lips and face squarely the acidic moonlight.

But a rustle of wings indicates that the celestial commercial is over and I am currently addressing thin air. What a nuisance these creatures are, all said and done, posting their "paradise" placards bang in the middle of anywhere!

Don't get me wrong, angels are all right in their place, but oh so useless when it comes to hard-core discussions because you can look right through them and their diaphanous souls when they tremble translucent chins and offer take-away heaven in a box. A slice of morality that gives you nothing but gas.

First the facts; you have a son and so have I. Your son. Juxtaposed against my son. And I remember that summer again. When the eardrop danced on your cheek. Some man placed it there, I remember thinking. Some man.

All I focused on then was your hands that wiped the vomit off my chin and chest, the tea that kept acidity and nausea at bay and perhaps your feet as you scurried all over my home and hearth, straightening, fussing, cleaning, replacing. I watched you from my bed, bloated belly blocking view. After all, you were hired to serve.

Any eloquence now is belated, of course. At that time I was the incriminating, mute prey you wanted me to be. Or else why did you move on and take those burnt-out eyes with you?

My whole world was crumbling, obsessing me with its cracks and strains; a second pregnancy, you see, and I sought you once again, someone to tide me over these unending months, to clean up after me. And this evidence – for it was that as you and your son trundle up the long, winding path out of the darkness – of further sabotage was unwelcome.

My husband's spitting image is my first thought.

"Is he yours?" I ask hesitantly, for I am fully prepared to kick-start my belief in coincidences. Anything can be explained away if one obtains the right words or talks long enough or loud enough or believe in a god, any god from the many out there.

Your glance is steady, almost as if the wait has been on your part and is now officially over. I hungrily gaze at the boy despite some faint warning bell inside my head going nnning-nnning, bidding me to avert eye. He stares right back. This boy of....

"Four," you supply, robbing intensely.

Ah, yes, now I remember how many years it is since I returned home with the detestable bundle of joy, my firstborn, and you had vamoosed.

My feet shuffle backward to the crudely concocted door. You follow me out, scratching your face, a matter of dragging broken fingernail down eggshell-cracked skin and all of a sudden the scraping surface of your skin is hypnotizing. Still I made my escape, for clarity needs six by six vision and there is too much failing light all around here.

"Kindly adjust," I am told everywhere, in planes, in buses, on streets, in families, even here in these private places deep in my heart where you've come calling in debts too close to the bone.

The night is long and cloaking, but it has claws I

can tell. Who knew what nook of the night would unsheathe them. Who are you to cross the night? I mean, who are you? Angels are asses, disappearing before you can ask for aspirin.

Your stricken face splinters and swims around me like photocopies of different sizes, as if that was all you awaited, my knowing, but all I knew at that moment was that this was a knowledge I could have done forever without, it so dovetailed with other not-knowings.

My head tilts up, sizing up the stars strung out like linen in the unwashed sky when a stampede from the opposite direction meets me formally. I wonder at the sudden influx of people, streaming against me, at me, through me, dancing violently, followed by a horse carrying a flowered man.

"Keep walking, you bitch, keep walking, or prepare to break out into blasphemous feathers," the anti-angel brigade bids me and I hurry along the thorny brambles. It is a con job, this paradise these prudes go on about. If my aches make them angels, then let the parasites out of my heart; I shall ache no more I swear.

"What use has goodness been to me?" I ask him from a roadside booth, clutching the phone tight, reading lonely messages scrawled on the pane.

"Where are you?" he wants to know while the pane tells me: "Fukking u Now."

I nervously toss the receiver at the booth guy and

collapse on a rickety stool. It comes upon me that I am no individual. Nothing as lofty as the sum total of this part and that part either. It is like I am composed of transient touch-me-not ingredients; a patched-up doll of mist and ditchwater, dripping with extreme virtues.

He appears in a flash.

"My husband," I greet without recognition.

He grabs my elbow, guides me back home, tucks me in bed, head aloft on a doubled up pillow like a balloon high in the sky, and fluffs out the cotton under me until they are wings of white. I blink, but no, nothing so topical as a tear is under manufacture.

"Drink up," he says, flashing the momentary white of his eyes at me. "You are fine now."

I try to swallow but the throat fights back. Sleep, however, has other plans, spreads over like a blanket, shoots morphine up varicose veins, rocks and hums, sends me scattering up in the air.

Even if I shake off this insidious, monstrous drowsiness, my body chooses not to obey commands, soul yo-yoing into a stubborn, insecure carcass. Downright creepy to be diluted by somebody's sneaky remains, to be inhabited bodily by a stranger and in turn to rent a stranger's shell, the incubus a violation either way.

It is the doing of those winged women; peeking and giggling at me from behind the curtain. Injecting soapy liquids into me, to cleanse me from inside out, clawing out mortal dirt. I'm so soiled and I can't fight anymore. In return they have condemned me to eternal rest with a flap of those wings in a sorority haze, have peeped into me and clicked pictures. There is an album somewhere of me plotting and snorting, and holding my real exposed prints in their hands, they blackmail, chasing me to Hades. And now, now they play undertaker, have me down gagged and bound in someone else's body.

But there is no marriage where they come from. They won't stay listening to wretched decisions that turn out all wrong in the end. After all, straying husbands bring on all kinds of debates. For. Against.

I know he is watching me. Behind these walls his heart beats, affecting endless patience. Crave quiet and it is granted with a vengeance. I haven't passed out in a drunken stupor; this is no happy hangover, because alcohol only makes me silly. Sense a bright light overhead, dizzyingly darkening the rest of the room. I want to crawl into the brightness and curl up within, mainly so I can look down. A foggy, unformed arabesque is somewhere around the corner of my eye, just beyond sight except for its tantalizing tail end. Could I follow it to its conception, do you think, trace it by its subterranean soul-droppings?

Bodies are known to go mute on you sometimes. Like now, when all feels transparent. I can hear no heartbeat, no under-wire skewers the downside of my breast, but there's a strung-out scent pervading this insidious nebulousness, like an unseen force about to knock at my door.

"Nothing will matter anymore," he vows as the milk dribbles down my chin and cramps unfold deep in my belly like well-kept secrets.

What doesn't? And when did they matter?

I think these words and I say them aloud but they turn against me on my lips. Try to shift eyelids, stir tongue to banter past the air squatting on them and lungs, when he plucks the pillow from under my head, the suddenness of his move accentuating the giddiness, sending my split-ends on a pendulous spree.

Paradise to Purgatory merely a typo, he whispers, "I love you."

It has the pallor of an icy sky, the pillow bearing down. Ignites anxiety if courage can keep up with caprice. Fingers clench-unclench on the pillowcase a second before the sky comes swallowing....

The trick is to keep breathing.

YOURS FAITHFULLY

"Okay," said the insufferable woman, squarely buttonholing him. "Just listen to me and I promise it won't hurt."

He had been about to go across and make polite noises of farewell to his hosts when this woman happened. She lurched out of nowhere with her bold grin and an over-familiar paw that nudged him compulsively.

At first he thought she was someone he had met or known earlier and forgotten but she began with a bright, "You don't know me and I don't know you. What's more I don't want to know you and I daresay you feel the same way. It is just that.... No, I am not drunk," she continued when he failed to maintain eye contact. "You won't understand but it is my duty to explain. You see, you are the only unattached male in the room. Now don't look so frightened. Far be it for me to contradict your coupling plans. I am here though because you are, well, alone.

"Somewhere in this party is the man I wanted to marry. And I don't want him to think I have no one. I mean I have no one but I don't want him to know that. The ego does not permit such honesty, you will agree."

He murmured his assent in a strangled sort of murmur.

"See, it wasn't like he ditched me or I ditched him. It was all to do with his family. Waiter, here. Thank you. What about you? Please, do have something to drink, too, or you'll make me feel so ... thirsty. No? Okay. Where was I? Yes, his family, though there is nothing remotely 'yes' about his family. Very negative people. Always shaking their heads at this or the other. His mother especially. Dead now, of course. All that shaking can't aid longevity, can it? Please excuse me while I laugh." She then proceeded to laugh as if he had just been achingly droll. "That's so we appear to be hitting it off. Your frowns aren't helping, you know. Very much like that woman who wouldn't be my mother-in-law. Not good enough for her son, apparently. Mind you, not the money. For my father was rolling in the stuff; he is in the fertilizer business though my brother has taken over now and cut me off without a paisa. How shit pays! But that's neither here nor there. What's here is this mama's boy I am

SHINIE ANTONY • 93

meeting after twelve years, no thirteen to be precise, if you don't take into account an accidental meeting in May. You must wonder if it wasn't the money then what could it be? It was," here she leant conspiratorially, her left hand taking charge of his shoulder completely, "my looks.

"Or lack of looks as that mother of his insisted. My son Greek God, she went. And this woman – that's me – black bitch. I am dark, I agree, but I haven't gotten any darker now than then. What do you think? Is it dark as in the night or just dark as in sexy?"

His nod was interpreted quickly.

"So I said, 'your mom or me.' More fool me. For no man likes to choose at gunpoint like that. But what else do you expect; I was an immature twenty-five then. Today," she sighed. "Today I would've handled it differently. Tackled the mother first and killed her with sweetness. They just feel bad, what with menopause and not being able to sleep with their own sons themselves. Awfully frustrating for them. And along comes a nubile youngster and they strain their eyes looking for flaws, hoping the split would occur sooner or later. I speeded up the split with my hysteria, played right into her hands. No, no, this won't do. You cannot stand so aloofly. Bend some more. Look happy, look down at my ... chest now and then. It has to look like lust or nothing. I want him to burn with envy. You think his white wife does it for him now?"

Her left hand trailed up to his head where she tucked

an imaginary wisp of hair behind his ear. When she spoke again, her voice had changed pitch. "There was no one else for me." It was a whisper. "And I thought how can there be anyone else for him? After what we had been to each other, I thought he'd yearn for me eternally as I would for him. That we'd meet occasionally somewhere and look at each other and I could smell the ashes of our burnt dreams at the back of his eyes.

"Now let's just stand here, unmoving, and stare deep into each other's eyes as if we can't wait to tear each other's clothes off. No, no, that won't do. Haven't you done this before? Hmmm. I think tilt your head a bit. Yeah, that's right. Now sweep eyes over me in that slanting position. Pretend I'm … what's your favorite dessert. Tira Misu?" She squealed. "Mine too. That's what I am. Your Tira Misu. Look at me longingly like I am in a glass case at Barista and you've left your wallet behind at home. You want me but can't have me. That's good. Go … od! So that's what it was, my one grand passion. Surely, you are going to say, surely ma'm you must have met someone else, someone who could have wiped away the bitter memories and wrapped your heart in the warm cotton-quilt of his love. Alas, I did not allow it. Love is a once-in-a-lifetime thing. Just because he married and spawned a dynasty in a matter of seconds doesn't mean I'd follow. Oh no, I was faithful to the last. Come on now, it is only a hug. No need to shrink. But quick, tell me, is he looking at us?"

A Dog's Death

We had barely sat down for breakfast that day when a strange whistling sound sailed down our fifth-floor window.

"What was that?" we asked simultaneously, staring at each other before rushing to the wide window. Heads from other windows were peeping down anxiously too.

"Oh, it is that dog," said the domestic help in a disappointed voice. A pavement splattered with a mongrel's mortal remains was a comedown for her. She would have preferred something gorier than a mere canine corpse.

We returned to our breakfasts with diminished appetites. The omelette no longer felt fluffy and the tea turned metallic. Everything tasted ... dog.

"Whatever possessed it to jump?" a next-door

neighbour asked, walking in without greetings or apology. "It was from the seventh floor. The whole night it yelped and yelped. Then at 9 a.m. sharp, it just jumped." He shook his head. "I have informed the building secretary. If it is not cleared up immediately, the stink will be unbearable."

"I am glad it is dead though. These municipality people do nothing about stray dogs in the first place," my husband grumbled. "Just last week I counted at least five mutts here. And then, of course, the more common they are, the hastier they breed."

In his bedroom, my son tried to keep his eyes shut, but it was a futile exercise. On holidays he is allowed to sleep all he wants and get out of bed at own whim, but the bright morning sunshine combined with the ominous thud from downstairs made further sleep impossible.

The maid went in. "You will never believe what happened. A stray dog just committed suicide by jumping from the seventh floor."

In a trice he was up. "I hope it wasn't Browny. Was it a brown doggie, bai? Oh, please say it wasn't Browny."

She led him ceremoniously to the window. "Look," she pointed.

"It is Browny," he wailed. "Someone has pushed her down. Now whom will I play with?"

He ran to his father. "Papa, why is my Browny still lying there? Why hasn't she been shifted to a hospital?"

"It is already dead. Besides, it is only a street dog," he consoled. "Have you cleaned your teeth?"

"Mommy," he exhorted next. "Do you think she is really dead?"

But I was in the next room and pretended not to hear.

He rang up his friend whose parents were doctors. "Could you come over, please? There is a very sick dog here."

I ran out, snatched the phone from him and spoke apologetically into it, "It is not ours ... dead.... Yeah, I know ... I am so sorry.... You know how children are."

Barely had I put the phone down when he made another call. This time to a friend who lived in the same building as ours. "Browny is dead, auntie. Can I speak to Shweta?"

"She is sleeping."

"Just tell her Browny ... is no more."

I was firm with him about having to go to the bathroom. Throughout the cleansing ritual he informed me about the erstwhile dog. "She has eight pups, you know." I knew because he had pleaded to be allowed at least one of them as a pet. "Of course, only two are left here." He spat some foam into the basin philosophically. "Who will look after them now?" A pause later, "You know, her second husband comes sometimes. But he never plays with them. They are not his children, that's why."

"Breakfast...." I began but he had already started down the stairs to where the dog lay. I followed in a hurry, running all the way down the stairs close behind to prevent him from touching the carcass. It was a filthy dog, after all. Who knew where all it had been. Besides his pyjamas were buttoned all wrong.

The dog lay sideways, pretty much the same way we had spied it from our flat above.

"Don't touch," I said urgently, but he had already bent down and scratched it gently behind an ear.

"Sleep all you want, Browny."

THE ANTI-LULLABY

Ↄ He burst into the ICU; two minutes to sane, half past it in a second. Latika's bare shoulders peeped delectably doll-like as that first morning when they woke up together after a night of tentative lovemaking and she had shyly scooted under the sheet.

"Supposing you spell out the parameters of infidelity to me?" had been her last words addressed to him, irises sparking in those fragile under-folds of flesh, a slender arm akimbo, before the door banged dramatically and, poof, she was gone.

He should have drummed up a reply or two, delaying her, distracting her, anything to hack at that beanstalking ire so that she'd never have driven into the downpour just to get away from him and his one-eyed reasoning, her foot jammed on the accelerator instead of his throat.

Her mother's pat made him feel more of a phony, thickening the air around him; the mourning husband, brand-new widower, a picture-perfect tragic figure that went so well with hospitals and cut carnations arranged in photogenic vases.

She squeezed his shoulder. It was this simplistic acceptance of hers along with a general gloom orbiting somnolent gingham furniture and child-bearing hips that Latika had sought to genetically surpass; the giddiness of an escaped convict's orgy in her determined post-nuptial gaiety.

He saw that her face was scrubbed with tears, tears that held on to life longer than her from the looks of it. "Tears are useless," she had told him when a promotion passed her by, "catch *me* using them."

An orderly came in as if on cue, pulling up the curd-white sheet over her face and competently tilting her into a stretcher en route to mortuary.

Shush, can't you see she's waking? he wanted to scream. Breath non-bailable, she is tipping a toe playfully into the sea-pool at Lonavala, her hair riding the bike's pillion-breeze till it's a merry carousel of curls he itched to clamber onto.

But no words issued forth, his throat was paralyzed, ditto eyes, guilt perforating glassy-eyed grief. Back home he marvelled at how affable even the newspaper sounded. Breeze wrestled the open pages to the floor and if he closed his eyes, they sounded almost human, the rustles as draught and the fan's blades tossed them about, akin to sighs of a companion, breathing in and out in discreet silence.

It was in this same room that she had found him, riffling through her open suitcase, his tanned hand setting off the pearly tones of cascading lingerie.

"Even your trousseau was never so delicious," he had sneered, all his suspicions now confirmed about her delayed period. "Just what I need; somebody's bastard baby on my knee."

"I don't know if I'm pregnant," she had sighed, almost inaudible. "It was just that once, he seemed so lonely…."

"Didn't it occur to you," he asked pseudo-politely, "that his loneliness is not your portfolio?" Then sharply, "Or was he your preliminary post-marital investment, money in the bank, so to speak?"

"It meant nothing to either of us, I told you."

He had slapped her then, as if the meaninglessness was what incensed him the most. That she could sleep with someone and dismiss it as an itch. That she had tasted another bed, another body and calmly walked back to his bed, his body as if, hello, where were we?

"She craves pie-eyed men. Preferably with lust. Preferably for her," he encapsulated, absently registering the car's rabid acceleration. Hadn't tried her mobile, savagely imagining her getting laid in implausible places and positions, a nymphomaniac marionette getting all her buttons pushed by passers-by.

It was her mother who raised an alarm that traced her mangled car to the ravine. In post-gangrene coma with tears and flies for company, nestled in wet membrane still warm from her body.

He had been systematically emptying her cleansers, moisturizers, sun-screens, astringents and sundry lotions into the wash basin, faintly frustrated by their viscous nature, bloody contemporary Cleopatra's bath of asinine milk, when the land-line, mobile, doorbell, sirens all set up a relentless pealing against the loud buzz in his ears, the blood dancing a livid sunshiny red through his veins, drowning out hearing, calling to heels a nomadic mind, snapping giant fingers bang in the center of his chest.

Ram Narayan's tryst with cadavers began twelve years ago when he happily and proudly picked up an attendant's job at the local morgue. His mother had been philosophical, "The dead need company, too."

Earlier he'd head straight for the semi-detached bathroom upon his return from the .hospital, a hot bath a must before he entered his home. But by and by this sense of hygiene blurred. Dried marigold petals or cloying incense no longer chased him to steaming buckets and mugs. A camaraderie had developed between Ram Narayan and his corpses, especially the young and pretty female ones and in one desperate instance an adolescent boy, softly effeminate with long painted nails and silver anklet bells.

They helped him get through long nights of saving for his sister's marriage, her three deliveries, his brother's polytechnic fees, a leaky roof and broken tiles and sundry other homely holes that developed in the threadbare, fraying tatters of his youth until one day he was a balding man with no companions or wife.

His first lover had been a pious middle-aged mother of three, breasts vandalized by cancer. Neither was he a callous lover. Taking the time to learn by rote the names on the tags, he stored away any precious personal details of the deceased that he happened to overhear. They were not a series of bodies but a marathon succession of succulent flesh merging into an endless sweetheart to whom he returned night and again.

Latika, he rolled the name around on his tongue; by the time dawn got in a dekko it would be a well-worn, familiar endearment.

First he locked the door. It had scared him, that one time he forgot and a relative had rushed in, thankfully too distraught to notice Ram Narayan's ankles entangled in what were a new pair of trousers.

Peeling off the plastic cling-wrap that had kept his Latika warm for him, he divested her of her only claim to modesty, feasting his eyes on the smooth brown skin, shadows from yesterday's straps punched into shoulders, the compliant comeliness and mild androgyny, chiding her for the last, brought up as he was on the prosperity that desi ghee parathas implied.

He then surreptitiously examined her wrists for slits, not wanting to be surprised like with that suicide case last year. Those gashes had meant blue patches wherever he touched the fair flesh, as if sky and clouds had exchanged colors on her countenance, and he had feverishly made up some story about the carcass taking a tumble during transfer though no one bothered to ask.

When he gently traced her lips with his thumb, he fancied a flicker in those lax nerve endings; Latika's answering smile he took for granted. Such was his belief in the liveliness of his lovers that he fell upon her mouth like a man possessed. Her lips he ransacked with the greed of a two-month celibacy, after all, young, nubile girls took their time finding their way into this room, his arms.

Murmuring sweet nothings, he straddled the corpse. That was when he felt the primal discrepancy, when the percentage of her that was yet to rigor-mortise gently began to pulse. He vaguely knew this needed investigation, but the alien pleasure that ricocheted through him as a result of the convulsion consumed his more immediate moments.

They screamed and rocked together and fainted in unison to be discovered later by a virginal nurse who prided herself on a chastity purely by default and could find no words to decipher the miracle or crime or even the disconcerting absence of clothes except by way of tugging at other duty nurses' starched uniforms and leading them incoherently to the morgue. For months the hysterical but firmly hymened nurse didn't dare venture near the morgue again.

Latika's husband grinned as cameras exploded in his face. Yeah, he believed in God and second chances, he told a news reporter. They were planning another trip around the sacred fire to reconfirm the validity of their wedding vows. No, he wouldn't sue the orderly; the hospital sacked him, but he had written him a generous check. As he told Latika, adultery had never looked so good to him.

ARRIVALS, DEPARTURES

"The charge, milord, is murder of wife's lover by husband in a fit of jealousy." The lawyer sat down then with barely suppressed smugness. He was a bachelor and even if he married, he would go for one of those plain women who sublimated their passion in the flour they kneaded or the kids they bore and, worse come to worst, if his wife *did* take a lover, he'd lay off nasty-looking butcher knives and opt for a civilized separation over afternoon tea.

The accused was led into the court by a police constable who paused twice, once to pose for the photographer of a local tabloid and once to scratch crotch, by all means a constitutional right in the Capital. The man had a two-day stubble and an appearance that conveyed archived sweat.

The charges were formally read out once again. The Judge, who had trouble keeping his elderly eyes open and was eagerly awaiting imminent retirement to snooze 24x7, roused himself enough to ask, "Guilty or not...."

"Guilty," interrupted the man.

He's jumping the gun a bit, the lawyer thought, tickled by his own sense of pun since gun was the weapon of choice in this case.

"Can you tell us, in your own words, the circumstances that led to that fateful act?"

The man tugged at his bonsai beard, as if after-shave was more on his mind than a confessional. He was remembering walking in on his wife and her lover, both bare-limbed and wide-eyed. A crime of passion it had been. What was there to explain?

When the silence in the court had stretched to a three-minute one, he broke it studiedly. "I am the manager of a tour firm, which means I travel a lot, mainly to lock into place bargain packages in hotel and trip fares. Meanwhile, my wife ran into an old friend from college and they decided to take up where they had left off. Naturally, I protested."

"By killing?" the judge leaned forward.

The man nodded. Wasn't it evident, he wondered? He had personally handed over the gun to the police on a tray.

"I'd have thought your anger would be directed at your wife. Why spare her?"

The prisoner pondered over any suspect sexism in this query until the loud ticking of the court-clock on the wall prodded him. "I wanted to kill them both, but she escaped," he owned up finally.

"That's a lie." A woman with uncombed hair sprang up in the aisles. "He is trying to defend me. It was me who killed the man. He was blackmailing me, you see."

The judge, arrested by the distance travelled by her upper assets into fully opening his eyes, nevertheless shushed her. "This is a court-room, ma'm, not a fish market. Anything you want said, you have to take the accepted route." He nodded sleepily at a policeman and adjourned the court for the day.

The room was pleasantly painted with sunlight, warm and insulated against the wintry wind outside, inducing a languor to the movements of the two lying in bed. Rays of the afternoon sun revealed a rumpled bedspread.

"What time did you say your husband's flight is?" the man enquired lazily, his fingers winding a chemically straightened strand of her hair.

She grunted. "Long time. Coffee?"

He opened a languid eye when there sounded the unmistakable click of an opening latch.

"I always lock up," she was saying as her husband's figure swam into sight.

The neighbors, who had been gleefully predicting

just such an eventuality, then heard one gunshot and two piercing screams that almost burst the eardrums they glued to the door.

"When I saw my husband," the woman earnestly explained to the faceless mob in uniform, "I realized how he would never understand that I was with this man only out of helplessness. He had been threatening to tell my husband, you see, and I was getting desperate. I could prove my intrinsic fidelity only by murder."

The unmarried lawyer got up laboriously. Each time a member of the opposite sex opened mouth, the dim wit was inevitable. "Is it true, ma'm," he asked, "that your husband and this man had almost become business partners once?"

She hesitated, glancing across uneasily at her husband. "I am not aware of any such history."

The lawyer turned importantly to the judge, man to drowsy man. "In the year 1981, the accused met with the deceased and signed a document to that effect, undertaking each other's debts. Here is a copy of it." He handed the court-clerk a piece of paper.

"One more thing," he said, "You say you remember latching the door, but obviously it wasn't."

She nodded uncertainly. "I could have been wrong."

"May be you wanted to be caught in the act, so that the blackmail could end?"

"I am not aware of any such…"

"Your lack of awareness is causing us some problem, ma'm," he said, setting off titters in the courtroom. "Your lover...."

"Don't call him that!"

He managed to curb his surprise. "You prefer that I refer to the deceased as your husband's ex-partner in business?"

"There was no reason for my husband to mention this to me as he did not know of my own personal acquaintance with him."

"You may well be right, but he should have, like all good husbands, mentioned something about a new commercial tie-up he was considering to tide Falcon Travels back to black."

Voice faltering, she declared, "I take no interest in business."

"Even your husband's?" the lawyer allowed an eyebrow to resurrect. "A business that keeps him so busy that you end up socializing alone or with ... old friends."

"Even my husband's," she said more firmly.

"Then it is a matter of indifference to you that the new partner was to be ... the deceased. According to the terms of the joint venture, all liabilities of Falcon were to be carted out of the profit margin in the company of the deceased. A strange MoU, milord. It was almost like the death was pre-ordained," said the lawyer, turning to the judge whose soft snores could be heard right unto the back of the court-room. Turning to the witness-box, he continued, "And this death leaves your husband with majority bonds of the company. It was precisely after he signed them over to your husband that the deceased … died."

She sat down with a thud and a court-coolie, this time female, ran over with drinking water, which she proceeded to sprinkle over the fainting woman's face.

Her husband had picked up the gun and pointed at self. "I love you," he said in a sepulchral voice. Three words he had uttered only in prehistoric honeymoon times. And she had started to grapple with him for the gun.

"Give it to me. Come to your senses," she exhorted while her lover quickly wriggled into his inside-out pants. The inter-locked seams had caught at his watch strap.

"I will kill myself," her husband declared with a marked lack of emotion. As he pulled trigger and as she intervened, it was the third of the triangle who slumped forward at the shot.

"Ohmygodohmygod," she had fluttered and manfully her husband had come to the rescue. "Listen…."

And she remembered belatedly, standing in a legal cubicle amidst total strangers, two facts. Two facts she had forgotten in the hurly-burly of hysteria. One, the casual mention of her old boyfriend by none other than her husband, who then proceeded to drop enough clues and inexplicable absences so she could catch up with *old times*. Second, when he entered the apartment that fateful afternoon, the gun had already been in his hand, pointing at them, hadn't it?

NEXT TO NORMAL

"There are no ghosts," everyone scoffed. And up until 1971, if someone had asked him point-blank whether there were post-death personalities, he'd shake his head as no questioner then vanished into thin air with a bang.

Plus, he wasn't the type to eavesdrop on the domestic help, not even when they gossiped freely about the previous occupant's sudden death in these very premises. Being a military nomad, he was prone to abrupt transfers, which meant moving in willy-nilly anywhere in the world with maximum wooden boxes and minimum fuss and it wasn't always possible to demand a house no man or mouse had ever died in.

The maids had at first mounted an imperceptible vigil for his non-existent spouse, then bravely came right out and asked, "Memsa'b?"

"No memsa'b," he announced, baffling the servant-quarters into a million instant legends on the cause of his Mrs's demise, each more tragic than the other.

Since the Mrs was merely estranged, this rather entertained him and he enjoyed hugely the mantle of a grieving widower thus thrust upon him. His wife had been rather a headache, what with having to watch her and wonder at the extent of her hostess-duties to male acquaintances. He cringed at the apologies and amnesia her extra-marital meanderings had caused him, since senior officer was god in the armed forces. It had been a relief when he walked in on her and goodness-knew-whom one day and could ask her to unofficially vacate the post of his better half.

"He will marry me," she had sworn at him at the railway station, standing by her haphazardly packed trunk.

"Who?" he had asked with zero interest.

"Major Chopra."

He had been hard-pressed not to guffaw. Major Chopra was the male equivalent of his wife and rather enjoyed his role as rooster. Him messily divorcing his old wife and opting for a newer model, which would start whining and wheezing sooner or later, was inconceivable.

Her subsequent postal plea for a legal separation he treated with the disdain it deserved. The very idea! Then Major Chopra got in touch with him.

"I say, old chap," the major began baldly over

subsidized whiskey in the Army Club, earwax spotting his sideburn like stubborn flies. "I'd like to marry her. Tie the knot. Make it up to her."

Asking for her hand as if he was her father!

"Sign those damn papers, I say."

He had half a mind to accede, so that Chops could traverse the cuckold path he himself had with such single-minded apathy. But divorce meant taking a public stand, to explain to family and friends, to furnish reasons and turn inside out the state of his soul, to abdicate the status of the Man Wronged. He had suffered the string-attached attentions of too many officers' wives with pug-ugly daughters to offload to take lightly his suddenly single status. Sex was over-rated and warm meals anyway he got at the mess; in short, life couldn't be smoother if he was a pupa sliding lazily down a silken thread to the butterfly stage.

The Bangladesh war came next. And with it arrived subtle and then overt pressure from top brass to perform high-profile acts of valour at the venue itself. Major Chopra, who did his best to garner sick leave on the falsest of pretences, was flushed out of hiding from a civil hospital and despatched to duty. Unfortunately, they surfaced right next to each other in what can only be called a coup of coincidences and even more unfortunately, Chops laboured under the mistaken impression that strife-ravaged territory would soften his stance toward signatures.

So there they were in the middle of what seemed increasingly like nowhere, in the belly of a highly secret undergrowth of Khulna sector in erstwhile East Pakistan to be postal-precise. The strain of appearing deeply absorbed in campaigns to superiors was amplified by this constant companionship and he suffered Chops like he would a haemorrhoid, with bad grace and secret grimaces.

When during an air raid, they had to physically operate from the same tent, he had tried to establish an immunity. However, Chops gave him no option but to react verbally to every hypothetical situation, virtually flushing him out of any metaphorical hiding. The raid gradually turned vicious till all dung hit the fan with a vengeance. A group of refugees was walking a tightrope distance into the inner recesses when gunfire shattered the uneasy calm. Chops, whose core competence outside boudoirs was never really clear, gave himself up freely to fear.

In the night he looked longingly at the unlit candle but went through his ablutions in the dark, knowing the danger they posed by drawing attention to themselves. As he sat with Chops, knee-deep in ration rum, there sounded the unmistakable rage of a nearby bomb that missed their bunker by a whisker. The men had all dispersed long ago, segregating and going their own way, scrambling over the borders, hither and thither like rats freed from a lab. There were just two bunkers now, one with the war correspondents cuddling their field telephones like newborns, whispering excitedly their so-called scoops, and the other with the two of them; both horribly aware of the posthumous medals awaiting them. Fortified with drink and danger, they dug a hole in the ground, prepared with buckets of green leaves for camouflage in case foes found them before death.

He lit the lighter, catching Chops unawares. "It is warm here at least."

Chops hiccupped, his reddened eyes darting rodent-like, visually rummaging the muddy womb. A faint smell of excreta hung in the air.

They heard footsteps above them and froze, fear penetrating the drunk's haze like knife via sun-kissed butter.

"Here is the hole," a voice said nearby.

There was nothing to it except shoot Chops in the brain and leave him strategically leaning with gun in hand as if in suicide; they were bound to ferret out the commanding officer and the mercy of it was that they would expect to find only *one* commanding officer and that too dead by own hand. Breathless moments later he heard the faraway rattle of the jeep but it was two hours before he could bring himself to unpeel from his extempore bunker, a hole in the hole he had got the men to dig for him in case just such an emergency occurred.

Oh no, he had never believed in the supernatural, not until he had picked up the pistol and aimed with point-blank precision at his sozzled companion. The doomed man looked up and in that split second before his brains splattered messily on to his boots, their eyes had *met* for the last time. That was when, fancifully enough, a Bollywood-red light travelled toward him from Chop's eye and ricocheted right into him, consuming him, *becoming him.*

Back at base he called up his wife at once for he had come back from Bangladesh a changed man. Literally.

He was now his wife's lover.

MATCHMAKER, MATCHMAKER

I had no business seducing the girl but sex had become a habit and at my age one does not deliberately hunt down morality. Besides she had bent over her chair, ass thumbing its nose, instantly bringing to mind my favorite position. By evening we were in that position, once, twice, thrice, and by next morning I was bored.

"Tycoon," she giggled, for she had read about me in the pink papers.

The mobile's burr gained momentum as she waddled over to trail a hand against my dark blazer. "It makes me look so fair," I could almost hear her think.

Saved by the bell. It was Kulwant, reminding me as if I needed reminding.

Dressed hurriedly, careful not to catch her eye lest

the bimbette took it as some form of encouragement. God forbid, she was one of those who imagined herself in love! One gets a fair amount of the type in the course of one-night stands; genetically conditioned to always arrive late, know last, wont to forever wander in a maze of platitudes, meander from merely ornamental to fully mental zones, leaving the mantelpiece so bereft. Tell them to kiss your ass and they file it under R for Romance.

We pucker up. Get the mechanics over with. Meet eye, look down at lips, re-meet eye as if to say hell, your lips haven't disappeared since I saw them last, slant nose and take it from there. One rarely melts into a goodbye kiss.

It was courtesy my driver's altercation with the hospital's parking attendant that I spied the girl again. She had driven up in a cab right after me and was now stuck adjacent to Jaslok Hospital. Dark glasses prevented our eyes from meeting and I allowed no change in expression. But in the long corridor there could be no eternal respite.

"Aha," she murmured, thinning her luscious lips with an effort, "This is office?"

"No, my wife."

Suddenly she whipped her blouse up, exposing breasts, boobs, tits, melons, jugs, knockers, whatevers. Your wife, she was saying, flashing her raspberries, is too staid for this.

Porn at the wrong moment is the pits. Skirting, I opened the door. Kulwant had managed to maneuver herself from the wheelchair and was now prostrate in bed. She waved at us weakly, only I knew the effort it cost her.

The girl threw me a look of pure malevolence, flew down the corridor, right where she came from; oblivion is my guess.

Closing the door behind me gently, I shrugged.

"Can't stand your loving?" Kulwant's voice slurred, her face expressionless due to advanced paralysis. It had eaten away at her mischievous grins and burgled the bite from her wondrous repartees.

I bent down, inhaled the baby-powder breath of hers. "Mmm, not loving, just the leaving."

CASE OF THE
DISSOLVING BRA

Her cleavage, he was sure, would be the pulp of an over-ripe fruit.

She was adorable, his junior at office and a married woman to boot. Not that it stopped him from perusals, throwing her sudden intimate smiles during some routine senior-to-junior meeting or turning to her with comments just personal enough to disconcert.

He had been told in college that his talent lay by and large in making women feel special, leading them to believe themselves in exclusive relationships with him. All it cost him were prolonged eye contact or not, for women either loved intense stares or hated them and it took only a few seconds to gauge type.

Like picking up a piston and squirting twin streams of delight into their eyes; they rarely question devotion since it equals their own for themselves. And if there was one-odd woman who thought he had an urgent thyroid problem because of bulgy eyes, he was also blessed with the ability to conveniently forget and focus on next please.

Catching her eye, he blinked twice in rapid succession to indicate that she had caught him lost in officious thought. He had great faith in his eyes – what had that copywriter woman called them? – ah yes, rum-soaked raisins, producing penile pandemonium amongst progesteroned pigeons. And he had great faith in his sense of humor, which was an added six inches.

No, this one was not interested yet, this woman with cellophane bra straps riding those dew-dappled shoulders. Must be happily married or did not fancy him yet, perhaps either or neither. Experience had taught him that attraction was only a matter of positioning – you just had to be that bloke across the crowded room with flexi-eyes, you were sure to catch someone's eye – he wasn't in sales for nothing.

Sartorially she was all suggestiveness; when she wore jeans, there was a bit of flibbertigibbet frill at the sloping waistband and saree pleats dived determinedly south! His nostrils twitched whenever she brushed past him; ah, the different smells of different flesh.

But he knew some women eschewed the mangal-sutra as a bit of archaic junk only to sport a mental one on their breastbone with the tenacity of a suckling babe. So he bided his time, spending an extraordinary amount of it decoding spaghetti straps, duct tape and straps in absentia, and sure enough as they worked side by side, averting a crisis one eventual day, he spied with a sideways glance the teardrop at the center of her cheek.

Gentleness was the key, he knew, so he held her gaze tenderly and invited her for a closed-door conference.

"Tell me," he commanded silkily and softly.

And she did, some eminently forgettable drivel about her husband's mother and her interfering ways.

"She is always going on about the grandiose proposals he had received," she sniffed. "It is not like I had no boyfriends, you know."

He was careful not to speak too much, to nod whenever their eyes met. He wanted to be everything her husband wasn't at that moment. And he was not fool enough to make a move way too early either. Just compassion for now, he severely bade himself, and that included keeping his eyes off breasts lolling on the desk between them like alternate bread rolls.

The next day he called her at home before she could leave for office. "Take a day off."

"It is okay," she sounded suitably unsure. "I'll come. There is the NGO paper...."

"Leave it to me."

Two months later he was planning a way to arrange something more intimate. Much metaphorical handholding had taken place, now it was time to fructify. He waited, humming this tune under his breath that got on everybody's nerves.

When she walked in, radiant in a mango-yellow saree, he was tempted to just proposition, varnish be damned. But he knew women and their penchant for foreplay, so keeping his gaze firmly on the back of her blouse where, wonder of wonders, he could still discern no bra, he called out her name.

"In here," he jerked his head at his office and obediently she walked in.

"How are you?" he spoke caressingly; voice ebbing and enfolding in an intimate embrace.

She raised big romance-novel eyes. "Sosososososo fine! You see my mother-in-law has left and he is back to himself. And it is all thanks to you. You've been such a friend, a brother really. How can I ever thank you? My husband is dying to meet you. There are such wolves out there, were his exact words, but too few gems. You are not going to believe this but some men would have just exploited the situation."

The Gem smiled uncertainly and collapsed back into his chair.

She cooed "thanks" once again. Then she walked out, subsided before her PC and blithely punched the keyboard.

"How did he take it?" asked her colleague, lips barely budging. "Not that you have any more leave left."

"Like a hooked fish, the little stud."

BRUSH-OFF

Priya swayed tunelessly to shush the baby, but it bawled away unabashed, pink lips asunder, seemingly forever. Manish's mother had called earlier and that always got on her nerves; her womb's VRS had Priya carefully sift her speech for propaganda.

The headache intensified, holding up her skull with hot tongs. Manish's uncle, who had just moved in from London and was still scouting for a suitable place to move into, whisked the baby from her.

"Teething I presume," he smiled, swinging high the baby, who shut up to enjoy the anti-gravity ride.

"How do you know, being bachelor and all?" she scooted over, her own lip wobbly.

"I was a baby once."

"So was I. But I could kill this one," she swore. "Or at least sedate him for a month straight."

"Hush, they catch the gist, these little tykes. Get his bottle, Lazybones, rise and shine."

So she rose, drawing the line at shining, and went kitchen-ward, upending the bottle from its watery bed and adding the requisite amount of milk powder and boiled water. A baby was tiring, so was an elder child and so was keeping house and if you added to it a pinch of socializing, PTA meetings, neighbors who dropped in unannounced and well-meaning relatives galore, the fatigue was mind-boggling.

Manish had joined MBA classes in the evenings, going back to office after that so that there were days and nights on end they never met and he became another voice down the phone-lines. Soon, but God knew how soon really, their golden future would arrive and she would ride away into the sunset with him. Until then, there was the baby and his bottle.

Baby slurped noisily, periodically throwing in little satisfied grunts in disconcertingly adult bass, and she began to plan dinner. Now that Uncle was here, she wanted to make an effort, pick up all her culinary talents and parade them under his NRI nose, but her supervision had ingredients rebelling, wilting, freaking in the frying-pan till they resembled nothing cook-bookish. He was sweet though, never complained, always insisting on taking her out instead.

"Tired?" he asked now.

"Huh, less than you. You were up most of last night with grand-nephew."

"At my age you need less sleep."

She smiled fondly. "I hope you never find a place of your own."

There was always something interesting to chat about and something exciting to do these days. She had surprisingly stopped missing Manish and was able to tell him without rancour on a day he expected an especially acerbic attack, "Your absence is with reason. Just a year more and you will be free. They'll understand, don't worry."

Uncle's presence helped everyone, not least the children who had resigned themselves to daddy gone and mommy snappy. When Uncle moved into the baby's room, it was bliss. He tickled the children, lullabied them, cajoled them into sleeping early and did the needful if they loitered late at night alluding to pee or drinks of water.

Her black circles and acne constellations smudged out and she smelt fresher than botanical extracts so that one night Manish was taken aback when she cited exhaustion at his standard, playful prelude, "How about a li'l fuck?"

And when he jokingly called her, "Your Highness of Dryness," Priya just went off to sleep.

She turned vegetarian, too, like Uncle.

"I think of chickens as parents or kids, of their lives and relationships and emotions, may be primitive and primal, but as real and throbbing as ours, and I cannot bring myself to enjoy them on a platter, socially unequal," she earnestly explained to him at a fancy restaurant, dodging his horny foot under the table.

When he brought her a dozen handpicked buds, perched prettily on long-necked stamens, she quipped, "Get me manure next time. More to the point."

Uncle and she mucked around whole day in the backyard patch and crowed incomprehensibly over pint-sized aubergines yet to purple or teeny tomatoes they'd never dream of putting into their mouths. Fertilizer bags leaned indolently against his kitchen wall, but when he pinched shut his nose, they shrieked with laughter.

It had pleased him at first to see his family getting along just fine without him, not clinging to him anymore. She no longer halted intimate proceedings, whenever he did manage to persuade her that is, to enquire earnestly, "Do you love me? I mean really-really," then sulking because he'd either hide a smile or pat her backside patronizingly, or more often roll his eyes, "not again...."

But it worked against him too, this intrinsic independence from him. Manish felt himself shrink, a dwindling he had no control over. It was like his voice came from another throat, less robust, until his voice had melted back into throat, clogging and cutting off.

"Beta," he called to his elder son, who was working feverishly on a science project, but he only looked at him blankly at the offer of help.

"Uncle has told me what to do. You won't know," he asserted.

The baby had started to imitate adult tone – it was only a matter of time before he set it to actual words – and taken to regarding him coyly as he would a guest. When Manish bent to tickle his chin, he ducked with a touch of frost.

Ambivalent about his family's newfound aloofness, Manish decided not to kick up a ruckus needlessly. So far, so good. Only a matter of time until he could relax, re-insert himself back into their daily lives, perhaps take them all for a holiday abroad. Yeah, that was a good idea. June would be the best month, when schools shut and Delhi turned furnace; somewhere cool and snowy with double beds and duvets and room-heaters. Must ask Uncle, too, he was being such tremendous help. Yes, that'd be a thoughtful, thank-you bye-bye gesture.

It was a rare night that he was home. Setting up own business was no picnic, as his sore lower back testified. But this late he did not want to disturb and chose to scrunch down on the sofa. He fluffed a cushion under his head and had just about settled down when the baby began to cry. Stupid with sleep, his feet automatically moved down the corridor.

Anonymously he watched Priya from the darkened corridor, breathing softly for fear of disturbing baby further or startling wife into an irretrievable "ouch."

She was already bending at the crib and taking the baby back with her to bed where Uncle snored gently and companionably.

VEILED

Niloufer had not planned on being a girl. It just happened that way. Before her there were boys and after her there were boys, but it was Niloufer's arrival that described them as before and after. From early childhood she had watched her brothers and thought herself one of them. Indeed, when at the age of eight, her mother forbade her from leaving home without a shawl, she protested. When she climbed hillocks in the dry desert terrain with her siblings, they reached the top much faster than she did. Even when she ran back from the school with them, this long piece of gauze stuck between her ankles, toppling her, making her clumsy.

Then her father told her mother that it was time Niloufer stopped going to school.

"What will I do whole day at home?" she asked, perplexed.

"Why, you will learn to cook and sew like me," her mother smiled. Niloufer did not smile back but by the time they bought her first burkha, she had learnt to cook and sew just like her mother.

One by one, the men joined the militia. In most houses only baby boys and old, unmoving grandfathers remained with the women. During the hot afternoons Niloufer never slept, but sat staring at the world outside. The rapt expressions, gesticulating hands, colourful clothes, flying feet ... of ordinary people going about their ordinary business. She could see them, but passers-by saw only a heap of black at the window.

"Don't let the horses in your mind gallop faster than real horses, Niloufer," her grandmother scoffed at her sighs.

Niloufer, whose sole sojourn into the world outside was to collect milk from the widow at the end of the lane, made the most of this outing by waking up early so all sluggishness of sleep could be shrugged off by the time the neighbor's cockerel grandly announced the dawn.

She would dawdle on her way up and down. Such a small lane really, but there was the makeshift road just beyond. Once she even spied a white photographer with eyes the faded blue of his jeans, her hand self-consciously going to her hair ... and encountering the black cloth. She remembered then all in a rush that no one could see her hair, no one could see *her*, and felt the sun's sardonic gaze drip hot wax, sealing the shapeless burkha around her like a shroud.

It was in their sleep that it happened. The women-folk had just slipped into their burkhas to go out and investigate the arrival of vehicles when Niloufer was dragged out along with other girls.

"Stop," her mother yelled, running after them, still pulling down her black cloak of modesty, but the men from another clan laughed and kicked her into the slush. When Rasoola's baby tried to crawl on to her, the man shot it point blank and roosters scattered about, crowing in confusion.

The girls took their cue from the one who dared to fight back, whose throat had been so casually slit. Wearing their burkhas from waist up, they waited until an hour later, when the vans revved and left with a macho swagger.

A flat wailing eventually broke out. Niloufer cautiously peeped through her eyeholes. Her mother was kneeling before the girl with the slit throat, lips moving in prayer. She knew what her mother thought, *hoped* – that she was the dead girl – knew because all mothers were hoping that.

Walking over, she whispered past the veil, the shame, the ball of stubborn spit that refused to shunt down the chute of her throat, "Ma, it's me."

OF NEEDS

His head lolled to a side and spit dribbled out from the corners of his mouth in endless bubbles, but Dhanalaxmi, or Dhana as her late husband called her, never officially acknowledged her son's idiocy. Whatever the exact medical terms of his condition, well-meaning friends of the family refrained from demanding them on the rare occasion that Dhana let down her hair, crossed arms to cause a mammary-jam right under her chin and laughed uproariously at their stale jokes. The poor woman, they knew, was worn out ragged by the constant care she single-handedly provided for this youth relentlessly self-irrigating like a top-heavy lollipop melting in the sun.

Flashpoint on technical details of his IQ was

reached only when she asked for Sharma's daughter's hand in marriage as calmly and formally as if her son was an Air Force pilot whose only drawback was having to fly those awful MiG aircraft that kept crashing down from the sky so thoughtlessly.

Doubts on her sanity were animatedly expressed in hushed corners of the street and Dhana herself was queried in various non-verbal options ranging from raised eyebrows to execution of swift bobs to the left or right when she approached from right or left, respectively.

Undeterred by these subtle signs of social displeasure, Dhana visited the Sharmas again, this time with astrologer in tow. What transpired there went largely unrecorded for consumption of the general public, which only witnessed the eventual departure of the two in good spirits.

Since the Sharmas were not as good at affecting deafness, well-wishers descended on them in droves like water-purifier salesmen, though being deemed victims they escaped sharper vitriol.

"Your daughter may be Spastic but does that mean she is any less ... normal?" trick-questioned Kumud-ben, the most concerned going by the expanding radii of her dark circles.

"Dhana has only asked us to think about it," Mrs Sharma defended, walking in with a glass of water on a steel plate in lieu of tray.

Kumud-ben, whose reputation as an anecdotal soul

preceded her, sipped the water with a sniff. People feared to cough in her presence for fear of reminding her of some long-ago TB epidemic.

"This is not the first time a cunning match was attempted. I remember..." Some time later she came to the point, "If you ask me, it is obscene, trying to palm off her sick boy on to you. He will be gifted to you like this." She mimicked Mrs Sharma's stance with the steel plate. "And you will pick a plain glass of water delicately as if it's *kulfi-falooda*."

If that was an intended slur on current hospitality it sailed completely over the strategically arranged strands on Mr Sharma's balding pate. "Kumud-ben, you have no idea how tortured we are over this. She is my daughter, after all."

"She is our daughter," Kumud-ben stressed, seemingly unaware of any moral repercussions of such a statement. "And I won't stand by and let that Madrasan swish her coconut-oil plait over our heads." She glanced at the intended bride, her twirl-dip motion reminding of a deft spatula in a non-stick pan. Imagine this girl taking on a kitchen or juggling, Ram and Laxman both forbid, babies at those lopsided breasts!

That evening at a jagran meet a lot of throats grew hoarse dissecting Dhana's nerve over loudspeakers' interference and intestinal rumblings courtesy seasonal fasting.

"A good mother will look after her son till she dies."

"Perhaps she is worried about later, you know, after she dies."

"There are places where such people can be placed," was the vague but firm response. "Marriage is not the answer."

Dhana's son, who had only been an inanimate fountain-mountain to rest eyes upon, now assumed the proportions of a juicy rumor. Stories like so many legends tumbled out; of his cunningness, of his supernatural gifts, of his perverted lust, of his legitimacy. Through this all Dhana went about collecting ironed sarees from dhobi, shamelessly haggling with vegetable vendors, reading magazines in the sunny patch ahead of her home and generally living life as if she never mapped a comical matrimonial union.

It was with the greatest disappointment that they collectively learnt of Dhana's subsequent decision, quite independent of the systematic protest building up around her, dovetailing with theirs.

"Silly cow," they mouthed to each other, smiling small, satisfied smiles in Dhana's direction. Some went so far as to offer assistance with the boy, if she ever needed, to prevent repeat panic attacks like the last one. "After all, what are we for?"

The Sharma girl went back to hobbling about on her terrace, like she was constantly turning around to ask herself something, and Dhana's son, keeping a safe distance from that terrace and the world, drooled and nodded all over himself, his mouth going drip-drip with the consistency of a leaky municipality tap.

So it came as a rude shock to Kumud-ben, who had dragged her insomniac self to Dhana's house for a bit of neighbourly post-mortem and was still adjusting a mustard dupatta matched exquisitely with her teeth, when asked to help masturbate the boy.

"There's a limit to my motherly affection," Dhana said.

PAPA'S GIRL

dear papa,
   i'm riting to thank for the crayons you sent me though ma sed you ought to know i was too old for them. i'm not really and am riting this with the blue one, my favritt.

here it is hot, pinku has lice and miss dolly is still my teacher. sometimes miss seys no need to come to skool if i don't feel like but ma sey no. now when she goes for work i am here alone. i am big she sey, that's why. when i wake if there is this silence then i know she has left for work. still i run to the bathroom door and look at the back to check if her wyte uniform is there. she sey she leaves in the morning but i woke once when it was dark and the silence was already here. i am happy for all those chillrun in her ward though they have to get injekshuns and things.

ma misses you. he can't see the sun, she sey, opening kichen window. why, i aks. she washed her face but it was alredy wet. are you blind? is that why they took you away that affernoon?

i pray to god for you come back but do you think papa that god really lissens? all my frends sey they pray and that's about fifteen of them in my class. there must be lots of fifteens in classes all over the world, do you really think god lissens to all of us?

if he is lissening, if you are reading this, come back. i promise to not sey about our game agin.

THE BACK-TO-BACK POSITION

*S*he was just thinking how real fabric-flowers looked when a spine's stiff angle caught her eye. It was so like ... oh, it was him! The passage of time since she saw him last had her gnaw at a handy lip before she resolutely walked up to him.

"Er," she said, unsure of how to address him. Once she woke with flushed cheeks, having dreamt of his disappearance. Now she dreamt of his company, awakening from the memory of embraces only to taste defection again and again, that newfound presence of his absence.

He turned around slowly, subjected her to his serious scrutiny and she was aware of the hurriedly clasped ponytail and smudged lip-gloss running like a wayward child all over her chin.

"I was j … just remembering you," she stammered out before the pause passed into eternity.

His eyebrows climbed so that she rushed on, "No, really. Look at those flowers. You got me some from Singapore and I thought you had picked fresh flowers for me at the airport."

"Water."

"What?" she asked, nonplussed.

"You put them in water," he explained and they both allowed themselves a low-key chuckle though at the time he had come out in an irate rash and ceremoniously seen to the wiping of the silk stems himself.

He must be waiting for someone. A horrible thought smote her; maybe he was cheating on his current wife, his pay-by-cash, plasticky, no-IQ-thank-you wife. This should make me happy, she told herself, and I must assist this rendezvous if I know what's good for me. It is that bitch's turn to suffer.

How *could* he love that woman anyway? How can he and his love come together without me and the child we created, a child he can never ever create in unison with anyone else except me, leave me out in the cold, sleepless, therefore dreamless?

"Coffee?" his voice broke into her reverie.

She nodded. It was at the coffee shop, as she idly stirred the hot brew that she enquired abruptly, "Why are you here?"

He kept his cup back on the table, far away from hers she observed, steepled his hands, finger by finger, before gravely answering, "To meet you." He had a newscaster's voice, flat and even, which was okay while asking someone to pass the salt but disorienting when it came to the subjective.

Though she had begun to guess, she was nevertheless rattled. "But I came to meet Sanju."

"Sanju asked me to be here instead. Happy birthday."

Her lips parted in a silent "Oh." For no reason really flashed a picture-postcard memory in her mind of the surprise party she had thrown on his birthday long ago. The cake had comprised three circles, a big vanilla glob making up the face above two smaller spheres of squishy chocolate boobs with almonds cast as obligatory nipples. She had baked them especially hard, so when exhorted to rub face in the chocolate chest, he almost broke his nose. The cake, all nine kilos of it cut with the precision of a brain surgeon, soon disappeared, leaving behind the exhumed skeleton of a pale twisted candle.

"Thank you," he had drowsily murmured, remnants of chest smeared on chin, when ribald, unimaginative cries of "bite" and "suck" had died down and the nipples long washed down with whiskey. Barely able to hear in the din, she had rotated face, his breath fanning her cheekbones until this very ear of hers presented itself as a mike before his mouth. And he had bitten it.

Passionately, like she was his last meal on earth. Rendering her, the indigenous snack, as bemused as him and glad that the concerned lobe was de-waxed and pierced prettily through the heart. She had had no idea then that husbands were subject to extempore evaporation, that far from gripping a beauteous curve, her feet were poised on a gelatinous edge.

Of course, then everyone else planned surprise parties for partners and she had soon tired of squatting behind dusty curtains and sofas, springing up to surprise and surprise a whole lot of surely unsurprised people.

Stir, stir she went now, staring into her coffee. Damn Sanju, her hopelessly addled adolescent son who believed in happy endings and connected every sob she smothered into a pillow to her long-ago divorce with his father.

"And you," she wanted to ask. "Why are you here?" Because if her blind obedience to offspring was well documented, in fact if the divorce petition was marinated with her maternal madness, his scientific detachment from sentimentality was equally legendary.

"How have you been?"

"That's a meaningless pleasantry and you know it," she snapped.

Again he settled cup and went through the digital interlacing ceremony, the fine hair on the back of his fingers momentarily diverting her. But before he could speak, she burst out, "I've been fine. Really-really fine," for he had ripped the skin off her soul and left her to rot back then like a mackerel on a rock. "I turn fifty today."

He nodded and she looked at him curiously. "There's something I always wanted to ask you. I don't know how ... I mean, do you ever, you know, feel nostalgic about us? Us, as in you and me."

He peered into the emptying cup and she was tempted to relate the crow's tale, the one where it dropped pebbles to bring up fluid levels.

"Sometimes," he said at last, not in any way satisfying her query. Nothing less than a breathless paragraph of prose without pause would have done.

"And are you happy?" Perhaps I am pushing it, she thought; he was averse to self-archeological excavations.

"Happy?" he barked and she was put on the defensive.

"I mean, do you regret anything?"

"Not the fights, I don't. Not your rants and raves and sulks and fits. I miss none of that."

"You know I don't mean that part." Her mouth wobbled once before she could add, "We had good times, too."

He gave a weary nod. "And what use would it be to God or man to linger on them."

"I was not ready for tragedy and suffering yet, that's all," she shrugged. Some people were able to calmly outstare bad news in the eye, go on with the business of choosing the freshest cauliflower for supper as they knew digestion goes on. Sorry, but she couldn't be cool and collected, all swallowed gulps and suppressed sighs, not without major medication anyway.

No. All she could think was to out-scream the screaming innards, to contain the splintering. Not think of the left auricle and right ventricle and the tightly swelling smudge spilling like so much ink, so that she had no control over the volcanic heart spewing lava and home truths. "Mind you, these were all things I meant to tell you some day, but not at one go, not this way."

When he didn't say anything she felt like a drama queen. "It wasn't all bad."

"It isn't all bad now either."

She leaned back. "So that's why you agreed to meet me. To rub your bliss in my face."

"No, just to please Sanju."

Sanju. "I should've dumped him with you. Then I could've led a life of my own."

"You couldn't see beyond him. In fact...." he stopped.

"I'll have some more coffee," she told the long-haired waiter before giving him an intense glance. "In fact?"

"I wished him dead."

"He was just a baby!"

"I know!"

They looked around self-consciously at other diners. Had they been too loud, they wondered.

"You were insane over him."

"Jealous of his own son," she pretended to announce.

"Being a mom did things to your head."

"At least it kept me from making a fool of myself out there. I wasn't the one being silly with some garish girlfriend. Come on, you knew she'd sleep with anything to climb up, the bloody creeper. You thought … god knew what you thought … that you'd become younger if you hooked up with someone in a pram. As if life is an earthworm, to cut into two halves. The whole world was laughing at you, if you really must know."

He swiveled with a savage sound, flicking his finger at the corner of her mouth. Maybe to get rid of the froth, nevertheless she shifted back, wary.

A part of her, the real her, flew right up to the ceiling with the remote control and watched the fun, curious how the two combatants in the arena would end this particular duel. But another part was stuck in a spiral, going up and down, up and down, caught in a mechanically defective elevator, bringing the bile to her unkissed mouth.

"And who tattled to the whole world?" he asked, voice dripping fake reason. "A gossipy old cow and no one with guts enough to tell you."

She crumpled at that. Agreed one cannot dazzle another for an eternity without fussing over face, looks, sagging and, finally, when all other options fail, developing what is loosely called the mind. Suddenly aggressive opinions were formed on art, on others, all at once she was caught up with what was hip, what was not, all at once she had become pathetic.

"I feel faint," she said in a panicky attempt to change the subject. Unfortunately for her she never fainted, not enough anaemia.

She had wanted to faint that day, too, when this man, who had babied her in his lap a long, long time ago, mouthed, "You can take it, you're a big girl."

Had picked up Sanju's gun from the carpet that evening and giggling wildly, had aimed it at him. Shot up, shot down with satisfying blood-curdling sirens and red-blue lights flashing. Ran behind the sofa and fired crouching from there. He was large, defenceless and flinching and she shot until the gun gurgled, then died. Damn batteries.

She wanted to sound like she couldn't care less. Hell, she *wanted* to care less. But her next attempt at verbal insouciance fell equally flat. "Is it like this for all women? A relentless courting that tapers off until the courting appears the other way round. I am the pursuer. The nag. The bully. The one from whom you should hide. Run, I'm coming, ready or not."

Clutching at his over-long forelocks, faking patience, he mocked, "Come on, we saved your face in all this, remember? You left me, that's our story."

Her legs turned to curly twigs under the table. She wanted to push her knees into a stomach, his or hers.

She so wanted to feel something besides this awful numbness, so wanted to feel some ... legs.

"Every married man is an extra-marital affair waiting to happen," she parried smartly, not wanting to see her smartness join the knickers around her ankles.

When he had flexed his calf muscles, preparatory to walking out that day, and because there was a heap of proof within her waiting to leap out and slash wrists, she had said in a raw, bleeding way, "Please, I love you."

Disbelief had displaced two eyebrows. "Love me less then."

"I will always love you," she had murmured evasively, not wanting love to be whittled down to fractions like devotion, erection etc. He had gone anyway. Leaving her curled in her own limbs, in her house-gown and loneliness, demoting the door to an empty rectangle.

She half-stood. "You are right. This serves no purpose." Then she sat again. "It is not as if now we can all shake hands and raise a toast to our newfound growth and say, 'we are immature no more, so let's meet up again,' can we?"

"There'd be no point."

His agreement aggrieved her. "There is no point to anything if you over-analyze. That was always your area, analyze anything to death."

"Don't you dare dismantle me," he snapped.

These things have to be said, screamed and gotten

over with she supposed; one's calm decision to walk out, other's stormy rebuttal, no marriage was complete without the drama of impending doom and its attendant lexicon. Script was on the wall, just aim and spout; everything a rerun under the Damocles' sword of divorce dangling overhead and if you were fracturing, better the heart than the face.

He had said that Saturday night, "It is not impossible to live without each other."

Words that plopped like scythes, thirty-two teeth guillotining the tongue in tandem inside her mouth as blood gushed out and drowned her rebuttal.

She had started to picture the two of them sleeping together by then, her husband and that woman. But that night, just that night, she wanted him to stay back, just that night she couldn't bear to think of them waking up on a lazy Sunday morning. Stretching toes gingerly, brushing the other's accidentally or deliberately, morning breaths mingling, voices thickening, his between a growl and a plea as he demanded bodily rights; a handful of thigh, a mouthful of tongues as they tumbled headlong into a singular entity, a hydra-headed demon with quadrupled limbs and a sandwiched gender.

She shrugged coolly now. "The discord and break-ups around us had lulled me into a false sense of calm. I talked myself into security, forever-hood and the law of averages; if it happens to everyone else, it can't happen to me."

"Now that it has," he interjected in his most rational voice, "others are automatically safe."

"All said and done, walking out is easy to execute if you put your mind to it whereas staying put is...." daunting, she wanted to say, thwarted only by a spit inferno in her throat. Oh, all that energy spent on staying absolutely still!

He gestured for the bill. "Anything else you'd like to have? Pastry, a salad...?"

A smile for no reason, perhaps? "None of the above," she said, finally managing to strike the light note she had been striving for. Does he overwhelm her with feelings and flowers, she was thinking. Does he gather the season of spring unto his arms for her? Does he pine? Oh god, I do not want him to pine, please don't let him pine. That is why I faked defeat, acquiesced in the end. A sort of "go-to-her" nod that he in his eagerness did not stop to doubt. I had thought I was being so clever, had reasoned that requited love would cure all ills, that too much of each other's unadulterated company would dissipate the essence. Of course I followed him in my car that first time and of course he went straight to her home, straight to her bed, straight into her skinny of course arms. I know because the only light on was the one in the bedroom and that went off in a hurry, too. Alone after thirteen years of marriage, after investing caring and sharing, not to mention youth, waistline and all my optimism, into a dud. Three months into forty-four and a husk he left me.

She could have, of course, turned tail and run to Mommy. But that would have meant smothering and oodles of tea, the total dominion of the damned. A long, pulled face inspired others to take you out of yourself, away from doom and gloom, which was your permanent postal address. They would question her desire to be so brainlessly his. And that would have meant the death of hope, too. For once she had announced demise, there could be no resurrection. A second marriage to the same man rising like a bloody phoenix from the ashes didn't happen to beefy women like her.

Her mother had descended with homilies galore. "After these many years of marriage, for God's sake, it is natural to stray. Young women with their fluff and flotsam are highly appetizing to the ravenous boys trapped inside most middle-aged men."

"But I've been a good wife," she had sobbed into her mother's lap.

"Which is why you are now the eunuch in his life. When he climbs into your bed it is to sleep, in hers he is a callow youth once again with raging hormones. In her bed he is immortal."

"And what if the tables were turned?" she asked him suddenly, switching to the present tense. "Would you want me, welcome me back into your life, into this marriage that we shared, if it was me who strayed, me who found heaven in the arms of another man?"

"Perhaps not," he conceded curtly.

Yet he barely realized the magnitude of her task, this task of forgiveness that did not talk of forgetting. She had been expected to seduce him back and then learn to trust him all over again, slaying single-handedly her own dragons.

"Nothing less than my death will please you!" he remarked, stuffing his wallet into his back pocket, but not before she caught a glimpse of the photo in it, of a woman laughing insanely into the leather interiors of his wallet.

"You were my man. You ought to have been obsessed with my views, my tits," she reparteed. In a way, she'd have preferred him to die. Not because she had been reluctant to be described as divorcee, but to deal with the insidious hope that murmured he'd be back, just you wait, he'd be back. Making polite conversation at electric crematoriums would've made far more sense.

They got up. At the foyer she dragged her heels. Let him leave first; she wanted to see his fancy car, the one Sanju raved about; besides she did not want him to witness her undignified scramble for an auto.

He put out his hand. It was no hardship, that handshake, but brought to mind the pujari's face, the one who had got them married, the one who first asked her to put her hand in this man's.

Her pain had felt fierce that day when she had shot him with Sanju's gun and she had automatically assumed her love for him to be fierce too. She had wanted to die, the gun was still in her hands when he was gone. Yes, she wanted to die, but at the same time she wanted to dress up for his funeral – did that make sense? – wear that silly skirt and despite the pushy nip in the air, abandon puffy wool. No kohl, kohl runs, and lips can go nude, which was in. Play smoking widow to his ... his decomposing.

"Bye," he called out and she flashed him a gay smile like a freshly minted coin, all shiny and metallic, sunny side up, before executing a purposeful click with her heels and turning to the flowers. They were placed in water!

"Are they real?" she asked but no one heard her. She lurched forward to examine the petals and before she could think twice she had snapped a leaf.

Sap oozed out. An attendant politely stepped toward her.

"They are beautiful," she gushed to him like she had just discovered she was Midas, "And they are real."

"Yes, ma'm."

YEHI HAI RIGHT CHOICE, BABY

The story I tell you today is from a kingdom far, far away where people were always divided into two over everything. If A said, I hate this movie, then his neighbors sold their assets to advertise its merits. They were passionate about their beliefs and demanded only an opposition to their beliefs for it made them believe in their beliefs better.

Here, at night time we see a girl get into a taxi. She can't articulate her gratitude to the driver. Lack of education, an innate shyness and the viscous wetness of her salwar, all combined to tie her tongue beyond a simple "namaste." Her husband sat in the backseat with her and he was silent too but his silence owed its source to a deep unease. He would never have knocked at driver sahib's door if it wasn't for the midwife's growing uncertainty and his wife's third trip to relieve herself in the chawl's latrine. The last time he had accompanied her and heard the rip of raw flesh as her water broke, and sweating, he had made it to the driver sahib's door.

"Don't worry," the driver told him now. His unease was palpable.

His wife whimpered. Her knees came up when she whimpered. Driver sahib's presence forbade him to touch her. That would denote a lack of respect. They were passing all the familiar landmarks but the impenetrable nature of the night and the absence of any hustle-bustle or people imbued them with the opaqueness of the unknown.

The wait for the bridge to open up until the Express train passed by seemed interminable to all three occupants of the Ambassador taxi. None spoke.

Though the bleeding woman had put her dupatta under her, she worried about the immodesty of leaving behind a soaked seat. The driver stared into the distance at the left where he would spy the bidi-tip red of the incoming train, which is why he missed the swinging lantern coming their way from the other side.

It was only when the mob had descended upon them, yanked open their door and laughed their angry laugh, did the driver recognize the danger they were in.

"Aha," said the leader, "What have we here?"

"A woman, sir," said his assistant, "whose stomach swells each time she is with a man."

The mob expressed mirth. Shoulders shaking, they pulled out the woman. "She has been careful," one said. "Look, no traces. How do we make out her caste?"

The leader came as close as her belly allowed and drew an insolent stare over her. "So?" he asked her.

She swallowed and took a step backward. Immediately his feet followed. "I asked her a question, didn't I?"

She shook her head.

"What does she mean, someone please tell me," he said with exaggerated patience. Then he asked her, "Are you married?"

At her nod, he plucked her elbow. "Then what is your husband?" He fished under his kurta and took out a penis that was fast losing its flaccidity. "Does his look like this?"

The man in the backseat of the taxi leapt out. "Can't you see her condition, you ... animal?"

"But I did not put her behind this stomach, did I? That was you."

The driver's door slammed shut. In the still of the night, it boomed like a bullet. "It is my wife, my baby," the driver said.

"What have we here," guffawed the leader at this comic relief. "Two husbands and one wife. Two fathers and one baby. Manohar or Mustafa, you tell me, sweetheart."

The woman's back was pressed against the taxi.

The man pulled his pajama up. It was difficult holding a broken bottle and an item of clothing simultaneously. "Just tell me one thing," he leered, pointing at his turtle-neck sweater. "Was his wearing this? Or was it a baniyan waala neck?"

"Mine."

The whisper belonged to her husband but the driver coughed over it. "She is my wife."

"Then who is he?"

"He is a neighbour. She is my wife and the child will be brought up like one of us."

"Kyon bey?" the leader turned to the husband. "What's the use us calling a curfew if you reach wherever you want whenever you want anyway?"

The woman moved instinctively toward her husband.

"So you are the husband, eh?" the leader asked the driver sharply. "You know what, I smell a rat."

He brought the jagged glass close to her heaving stomach, which suddenly seemed to cave in and she emitted something guttural.

The man blinked. "Tell me quick. If the baby is one of us, it needs to live. Tell me which one of them is your husband? If you won't then I have to bring this down on you, you understand, don't you?"

She understood then. The frozen hull of her

reasoning crumpled and she stared at her husband. Then, deliberately she walked across to the driver.

"Why didn't you say so earlier and save us all the trouble. Go, sister, have your baby in peace. Call it after me."

As the taxi zoomed away, she determinedly kept her gaze ahead.

So, tell me, was she morally in the right? As a wife, is she entitled to any fate except that of her husband's?

As your Betaal, it is my duty to warn you that if you speak a single word to break your silence, you will find me hanging upside down by the cemetery's tamarind tree. On the other hand, if you choose to keep quiet despite knowing the right answer, I will blow your brains out.

HOMETRUTH

"You mean he won't budge?" The soldiers were nonplussed.

"Does he have firearms?" one asked loudly.

Even then his voice was barely audible above the gushing tides.

"Not that we can see. He's barricaded himself under the bed. Let the floods get him I say," shrugged a young recruit, face nicked by sharp blade in the groggy darkness of dawn when the siren jolted them out on current crisis mission.

Meanwhile, the river continued to fret and froth. Waves swirled higher and higher, their foamy moustache visible from afar. The river had exhibited fury before, but never threatened to wash away moorings like this, the commander thought, directing his men away from the hutment, the one with the stubborn inhabitant, to other rescue operations. After twenty minutes of cajoling and bullying the determinedly hidden man, the soldiers were exhausted.

He made an impatient noise and returned to the gaping hole in the wall where the window had been. They had torn it open earlier to visually locate the man. Dark gray swabs swam before the commander's eye before his sight took him on a dim tour of the room. Rags were spread on the floor to soak up the seepage, a kerosene stove stood upturned, paws in air, and on the wall was hung a woman's picture, the dried floral garland around it suggesting recent mortality. There was nothing to suggest the man had live company in there.

Picking up the megaphone, the commander deliberately let his threat boom into the tiny room, "This is the last warning. If you are not out of your house in two minutes, we will have to use force."

His announcement ricocheted off the damp walls, the man seemingly deaf.

"Why won't he listen to us?" muttered the commander, eyebrows gnarled. "Break open the door," he ordered.

"Sir…?"

"Now."

Two soldiers cradled the concrete slab, used as an impromptu bridge, to unhinge the man's door. On the door was a divine invocation with coloured flourishes underlining the inscription. In one heave it curled into a million wood shavings.

With the door gone there was light enough in the room for them to make out that the man still crouched under the bed.

"We are here," the commander said, feeling his way into the hut, shoes squelching muddy water. "Where are you?" he called out, sitting abruptly on the low cot so that he bumped into some upright part of the man beneath.

Picking up the tattered sheet he peered under. "The river is rising fast, idiot, it will get you before you sneeze." As he bent over the commander could feel his heart thud uncomfortably against his collarbone. For some reason disobedience always whooshed the adrenalin up his spine, sent it roaring up his ears.

"Coming or not?" he asked, waving the nozzle of his licensed gun under the dangling end of the sheet. The sound of the river was getting closer and weaved into the commander's ire with the situation, his job, this man.

"I'll shoot him in the leg and haul him out," he thought, knowing enough to shoot harmlessly. Intending at least to shoot in the vicinity of the man to detach him from the rubble on the floor, he stood up and walked back. Suddenly he stumbled on a mound and went sprawling into the moist mud. Dazed, he sprang to his fours, looking around for his gun that had gone flying from his hands. A hand shot out from under the bed and in a trice the gun was being waved at the commander.

Flattened to the ground, the tip of his wet shoe resting on the mound of muck, he met the eye-level gaze of the man under the bed for the first time.

Both stared silently until the man spoke in a voice guttural with disuse, "Get off her grave."

THE WEDDING NIGHT

She sat demurely on her temporary flower-bedecked throne, embarrassed by the money in little envelopes being pressed into her hands. But she knew they would be handy for her mother, who had taken loans from all and sundry to execute the wedding. Her new husband was laughing loudly and she caught the stale whiff of toddy when he turned to her. She inadvertently shifted back and he had leaned forward deliberately to breathe mockingly into her face. "I am your husband," he said and she was taken aback by the intimacy, unsure about its application in the personal context yet.

After the reception they got into a hired car. "No AC," he commented, hand extending idly down the seat.

She quickly launched into an explanation, absolving her mother.

"In the Gulf, no car without AC," he said, staring out of the window.

"About my coming with you Amma said…."

He threw up his hands. "I'll try I told her. It is not easy to arrange for visa etc. These things take time and I am not the sultan there, you know."

The taxi dropped them off at the only two-star hotel in town. The room had been booked by her mother only last night; they had hoped he would see reason and agree to celebrate the wedding night in their small but tidy house. "I can always move in with Chinamma," Amma had said.

But he was insistent. "My friends will laugh at me." He had said the same about putting up his friends who had come down for the wedding. And the same about the dowry. "It is not for me. But what will others say if I marry with no dowry."

Amma had nodded, the desperation in her eyes carefully banked down, and booked two rooms for his "office" people for four days and a slightly more expensive room for the couple for one night.

"Very low-class area," he pronounced upon alighting from the taxi.

She pretended not to hear. At the reception they were accorded knowing smiles. Honeymooning couples were rare in the hilly terrain of Wynad; they were usually hidden in homes or smuggled out to nearby Ooty or Munnar at the dead of night.

In the room, she changed into another gold-bordered half-saree, but he shook his head. "Wear this."

"This" was a red synthetic net tent in lieu of nightly attire and she went into the bathroom to duly don it. When she came out, he was smoking near the window. She sat primly on the white-covered bed's edge, feeling like spilt blood.

"I have a lot of debts," he broke the silence.

She knew what was coming. Demands for more money. I won't allow it, she thought.

"And these Arabi sheikhs are money-sucking bastards. You are understanding, no?"

Unsure, she nodded.

"They were there at the wedding."

She vaguely remembered some men with headdresses.

"I have called them here. It will look odd if we don't eat dinner with them." Before she could react, within minutes it seemed the "sheikhs" were in the room and all men, including her brand new husband, were soon in high spirits. Chicken drumsticks were ordered, so was ice cream and liquor in branded bottles. A bit of each was fed to her, forced down her clogged throat. She tried to gracefully retire, but the room being just one and tiny, eventually she dozed sideways.

She woke with a start, choking, in the dark. A man,

she couldn't make out if it was her own husband, was atop her, heavy on her chest, squeezing the air out of her. Breathless, stupid with sleep, she tried to shove him off, but a hand clamped down her screaming mouth and consummation was hurriedly completed. Then the nightmare consolidated as the weight on her chest was replaced and replaced again. It hadn't been her husband, she understood that much, and it wasn't her husband now either. He was snoring on the carpet; she had visually located him some time ago in the dark, her gaze ripping into him along with convict gasps and screams.

A long while later, long after the guests departed, he stirred. Jack-knifing into a sitting position, he turned to her urgently. "They will stop at nothing. It was a question of my life. And they'll do anything for a virgin."

Suddenly he threw himself at her feet, sobbing incoherently. "Only you could help me. You have saved me from death. You are my saviour."

When she sat dully without replying, he hesitantly touched her hair. "You are a good wife."

FIRST PERSON SINGULAR

It is the ageing process – I don't know whether to go in without a fight or touch up my roots – but suddenly young men everywhere seem tasty. Tasty to look at, tasty to talk to, to eat.

"It is the last flare-up of the hormones; libido going down with tail a-blaze. A mid-life crisis," my mirror mocked as mirrors are wont to. Still I bend to that gray strand of hair, that tiny crow's foot, a crease here, silvery stretchmark streaking a lightning across my stomach there, for ageing is the very bitch unless you are hooch.

I have been a typical wife and I haven't. I mean I have been faithful to two men almost from the first day of my marriage. One, naturally and boringly, is my husband, handed over to me by his mother with a "mild detergent, lukewarm wash only" tag pinned on the label.

The other was this boy who used to come to Father for tuitions. In a sea of gawky students, he would meet my eye shyly but surely, as I pretended to check Father's papers and pens. I had only been trying out these budding wiles cheaply on the house, not consumed by anything remotely meaningful then. It was the wedding that woke me to the fact that feelings did not fall into place or pliantly acquiesce. It was only in hind-stereo that he seemed a haunting melody.

The day before my marriage, he was there in my room and all of a sudden the hustle-bustle fell away, receding from the corner I stood, anticipating I do not know what. God knows, if he had said, "let's elope," I'd have giggled but not skipped forth hand in hand anywhere into the wide world or even up to the lavatory with him. My priorities were pretty much predictable for my years, seldom at variance with proprieties of the day.

As a representative of all the tuition students ever taught by Father, he handed over a gaily-wrapped parcel, some really loud curtains I could hang nowhere. I took it, our fingers brushed perfunctorily and we smiled, carefully keeping our eyes out of each other's. It was on my wedding bed, sitting alone and anxious for the first time, that I allowed myself to recall the brush, the smile, the look, swallowing sudden regrets. Quite simply, I was a woman in love from that night on, only unmarried to him. I knew the names of the babies we'd have – their fingers brushed me sometimes in the dark – but with my own husband I felt a philanderer.

Two men; my eyes opened to one, and if I closed eyes I was with the other. I felt, fancifully enough, like a mermaid snapped in a seashell with the roar of the waves crashing in my ears, tossed pell-mell on treacherous surf between two faraway shores.

Happily married? Though I say I am married, I can, will, would, could never look you in the eye and say happily married. There's something to be said for unrequited love though, keeps you on the straight and narrow.

I'd hungrily listen to any tit-bits about him thrown my way on rare visits to Father's house. He had got the gold medal he craved, joined the IAS and married a gross woman with adjustable mandibles from one of those new-money families we aristocratically poor ones are always bitching about.

For long years this grand and misplaced passion took me by the hand and walked me sedately down the visible marital pathway and, to all who spied, spouse was my singular preoccupation. Then the children took over charge of my body, my thoughts, my worries and fears. But there were still times when maternal or wifely concerns siesta by the side of my brain like slothful alligators stupefied by too much sun and I am aware of a me, especially after the man I thought mine remarried two minutes into his first wife's demise in a road accident. Even Maggi noodles take longer to cook, whatever the ads may say!

By and by came that dangerous day when knives and razors caught the light, ropes swung meaningfully and buses swerved for me. I walked out of home this morning with no particular thought in my mind. The sun is shining and I am inclined to make hay, to do away with my own two hands, a sort of self, a sort of me, especially when the heart happens to be breaking on a sunny day like this.

You see, it had occurred to me by then that the core crisis could be averted by the simple expedient of having an affair. I scouted high and low for a lover. Which is somewhat like taking an apartment; you look it over for comfort and luxury, status yet privacy, in your mind are the myriad adjustments and cost-effectiveness of a new lick of paint, curtains, proximity yet distance to the main road where cabs are accessible for a getaway and T-shirts that'll look good on either of you.

I zeroed in on an acquaintance and did some serious flirting until one fine day he just stopped running and turned around in his kitchen. Two dishrags pinned on the wall behind made it look like he wore a cape and he hugged me slowly, as if there were a hundred prescribed ways to hug and perhaps I preferred the thirty-second. His hands were not unpleasant, but neither were they absolutely necessary. On me, I mean. On him, I daresay they were of considerable use.

When my breasts failed to roll to the ground with a resounding crash, he tightened grip and watched my face carefully, seeking extravagant compliments or at least minimal reassurance. Leaning against a stainless steel washbasin, I promptly affected ecstasy, which though politically correct seemed to exacerbate the misunderstanding. We were consenting but unfortunately un-aroused adults and the most forgettable small talk would have ensued if his wife hadn't rescued us with an "Ice. We have run out of ice." It was with intense relief that we sprang apart.

Never nudged another shoe I can tell you. Now I was on the lookout for that dog called Chemistry. Oh, I'd rather stick to monogamy than worry about eye contact during oral sex or etiquette while returning a man's forgotten Jockey's. Nothing is worthwhile if it doesn't pounce upon the heart, animate the pulse and generally crank up the juices. It was a long wait that I sat out, contributing directly to the diameter of my ass and per se petulance.

Sunday papers say women are having affairs left, right and centre, and I feared they had taken up the last available mate, so imagine my delight when passing around snacks at somebody's house, my finger brushed against a hairy knuckle. Hello! I thought, teeny bombs imploding in my blood stream.

It is mandatory here to describe him physically I know but it wasn't like I had much going for me in the first place. I invented fictitious details to gloss over the banalities of upbringing, to glamorize my past into a more palatable one, into a more hot me. Though this man, like all men, was too busy talking about self to delve too deep into me. Did he really imagine I wanted to know everything about him? Of course, I listened. So? Listening is feminine and nice. It keeps the talker at your mercy. While he talks, he looks at you and unknown to him his pupil clicks pictures of you, so that even in sleep you haunt him with your big "interested" eyes, until he presumes he remembers you from a past birth.

"Am I boring you?" he'd ask politely, while my vacuous stare enveloped him.

And I'd shake my head, for such queries are mere formalities. All women know that. Your yawns may meet at the back of your head, but God forbid he catches on, this happy conspiracy against People of the Phallus.

I began to fear that all that conversational catharsis would replace raw passion, and imposed on him a chatter-celibacy. When he telephoned, I'd invent mysterious excuses to disconnect; song in my heart, dial-tone in my ear. When we met, I'd dumb down verbally, giving little away, retaining potency and intensity for this time I did not want to be beaten, pipped at the post. I wanted to go all the way, pop my adulterous cherry, get with it and most of all get over the two uncaring men in my life.

The opportunity to cheat on my husbands came sooner than expected. On a picnic minus kids at a scenic spot, when all gingerly left in a rickety boat for a two-hour trip, I pleaded nausea and he took out some "urgent" papers from his briefcase. Then we waved at the others till the boat was a bobbing dot in the distance. To my appalled astonishment, ignoring my tendency to lapse into loaded silences, he actually sat and spoke!

That was an hour already wasted till I came to my senses and resurrected from my sulks to seduce him anew. Perhaps I had left it too late for the physical act, since he was ensconced in his familiar world of words and more words.

As I let my eyes linger boldly on his body, on the molecular mass of masculine meat before me, I was assailed by sudden doubt. Gay! He must be gay, I decided in a homophobic rush, loath to doubt my own suspect charms. Why else wasn't he picking up the signals, my hand?

I confess I began to lose steam. Together we had explored every crevice and cranny in his conscious conversational collective, we had left nothing unsaid or unheard. But when the boat began to dot the river again, he groped me urgently, one swishing sweep with a window-wiper hand. My smile virginally whorish, like a nun's with trained horses in porn flicks, we hurried over to our respective spouses and friends as the boatman jumped out and manually tugged at the rope.

The husband, trousers soaked to ankles, took my hand as he clambered out to the bank. "Did we take long?"

"Too long," I never miss a conjugal beat.

"That's an insult to my husband," yelped my friend. "After all, he was here to take care of you."

"He was wonderful," I gushed to her, as we walked companionably, arm in arm, secluded from the rest of the crowd, toward the makeshift pier where cold drinks were stored.

"He didn't make a pass at me," I joked to appear friendly and, above all, normal. If I intended to sleep around then normal was what I wanted to appear.

"Oh, I know that," was her casual response. At my raised eyebrows, plucked to within an inch of their existence, she elaborated, "Not after his prostate cancer."

BAD-HAIR DAY

Thank god his forefathers had left him with enough landed property to lotus-eat for four future generations.

"Babuji, dinner."

That was his crispest-tongued daughter, Amara, the one pushing thirty and not one whit bothered with talcum powder or a bit of homemade kohl or, for that matter, the frill of a few extra words.

Must ask that broker chap to get cracking or she'd be left on a creaky shelf in his ancestral mansion and where would she be when he had croaked and those sour-faced daughters-in-law took over. No, did not bear thinking about. These were the times he missed his late wife. She'd have known what to do, indeed not let things slide to this in the first place.

"Babuji," called his daughter from the doorway, voice dipping warningly and he got up without further dreamy ado.

"The boy is in foreign." The marriage broker displayed over-sized frontal teeth. If you laid him right down on the kitchen mat, you could grate coconuts off those sharp, ferret-faced teeth, so visibly social were they, Amara thought.

The eldest daughter of the house, expressly advised by father, opined, "The cash transactions are what bother. You of all people know, Broker Uncle, how educated she is. Double MA is not common now, is it? Almost a PhD. We do not want a crass commercial transaction."

It was with great investment of time and debate that they settled on a suitable sum. This was still large enough to frown up the foreheads of the three sons of the house, who were of the opinion that Amara could hang around the house indefinitely, nursing father and their own sons in turn as most plain women of good breeding did.

But the old man was adamant. He knew he could plan no pilgrimage or even manipulate moksha with such a large burden hanging over his head; an unmarried daughter was a ticking time bomb, everyone knew that. The only hitch was the immediate availability of the would-be groom whose vacation plans in faraway Manchester were followed with great interest in this remote rural household.

"Must be a big shot if they can't give him leave at short notice," Babuji surmised, wiping droplets of buttermilk from moustache. Still, preparations did not begin full throttle as the formality of boy and girl seeing each other was not over.

"My son," the boy's father then descended on them with considerable pride, "would never refuse. He will blindly marry uglier girls, legless or with bigger humps on their backs if I said so. He is most obedient."

It was with great trepidation that Amara allowed herself to dream, following the announcement of this virtue. A big, bulky woman of twenty-nine does not readily abandon herself to fantasies reserved for smaller, petite, diamante-nose-pinned sprites.

Every morning the head-maid lathered her with a special concoction made of saffron, turmeric, milk-cream, freshly squeezed lime juice and gold-water speckled with silver; this would lighten her skin. An egg was religiously mixed with her tresses and henna soaked overnight, eliciting unsavory comments from sisters-in-law regarding the ready availability of eggs to spare for her skull.

The said skull was in time inundated with unpronounceable, unfinished thoughts and doubts and Amara's usually serene expression gave way to a crafty, knowing sensual curiosity, documented by the sisters-in-law who could only speak about it anymore, as rapid breeding had converted their bedrooms into child-riddled chambers of celibacy.

The wedding date was fixed and the date, like all other dates, approached inexorably until eventually one day it actually arrived. The groom arrived the previous night and the bride had not slept the entire night, having sat up with a smelly facemask and half-formed conjugal fears.

The sisters-in-law condescended enough to teach her a trick or two in hair-care; whacking a hard-on into the newly cut fringe above her forehead, cleverly arranged to veil its unfeminine broadness.

The ceremony went off well as the sisters-in-law – who believed implicitly in PR – went about personally serving guests and smiling and crying alternately, in ecstasy at the people streaming in and the thought that their youngest nanad would now disappear into a stranger's home, respectively.

When the wooden palanquin was lifted, they broke into loud wails, alarming their husbands and impressing Amara's brand new in-laws. A girl who came from such a loving home would look after them like an angel!

The wedding night went by too fast to be documented here; a hurried coupling, a short-lived scream, a grunt and then it was morning. By the next night, Amara bid goodbye to her bridegroom, still unsure, still waiting to be unbelievably happy ever after.

"Very little leave," was the impressive excuse.

Amara soon settled down to serving her new family. The kitchen was where she spent most of her time, cutting and chopping vegetables, which were picked up and scrutinized for symmetry and size. She passed tests and time in this suitable manner, virulently domestic by day and somnolently wide-eyed at nights.

A year went by, then another. Her father went to Hardwar and came back. Meanwhile precisely six letters had been exchanged between Amara and her husband. In the last she had made bold to suggest, "I yearn to be a mother like Kukku-ben and Bindu bhabhi," and now waited breathlessly for the response to this postal pass she had dared to make.

It was her father, when he came to deliver the politically right prasad at her home – reared as he was on traditions that forbade him to taste even tap-water at married daughters' homes – who raised doubts over his son-in-law's absentia.

"Passports can be gotten like this. What problem are you talking about? He has his green card, then?"

The father-in-law explained patiently, "He will come soon and then take her with him. Two years is not a long time to get to know one's in-laws. I am her father now, don't forget that. It is my duty to worry about her."

Amara met her father in the courtyard where his cart waited.

"Babuji...."

"I have told them to send you to England as soon as possible," he said brusquely.

"Why are they keeping me here and why isn't he coming to take me or send for me? I don't understand. I'll kill myself...." she said, tears rolling down her tanned cheeks.

"Sshh," said her father kindly. "Trust Babuji."

Finally it was he that bought her a ticket and sent her with a pimply youth from their village, bound for Liverpool. They were to both get down at Heathrow and go by road to Manchester first where he would dump her like an unwanted parcel and then make for his own destination.

Amara's brothers and in-laws protested the decision and up until the flight took off they elaborately sighed, shook heads and looked tragic. And up in the sky, Amara herself wasn't on cloud nine, what with the blank silence that had greeted her letter on her impending arrival to husband. Still, she consoled herself, it took ages for the post to reach; all his replies had been at an overfed snail's pace. She had his address; all she had to do was land up there and watch the pleasure and surprise dawn on his face. She hugged herself in the excessively cool air of the plane at the sheer finality of her journey's end; she was a married woman, going to her husband's house and that was that, she thought, patting her cranial puff into place carefully.

Of course, he was already married. There was an Irish "Mc-Patel" nurse, petite with stillborn breasts and pale freckles they could spot over the fence. Fortunately, her accent delayed comprehension or Amara would have toppled over the wooden fence in dead faint. Her spotty escort chewed his first gum impassively, any relishing strictly private, as the white woman and Amara hammered out details of relevant home-truths.

The fireworks from a long-ago wedding revisited her ears along with this new explosion, so that Amara winced, going partially deaf and bilious on the spot.

"What I do?" she asked, back to her world of fewer words, only the necessary ones.

The nurse shrugged. Her night duty began in two hours and the babysitter was late again. This coloured woman claiming to be her husband's wife, obviously some tricky Indian misunderstanding, was needlessly holding her up.

After she had driven away and Amara had watched minutely the whirlpool of dust from her four separate wheels settle down, the youth urgently cleared his throat. She turned to him.

"The gum," he explained, gargling it out.

They sat by the impromptu pew till dusk brought her husband's car down the road. Amara watched him get down, his shoulder blades held at a stiff angle like she remembered from the wedding album, and glance at them cursorily and do a double take. This reassured her, at least she was visible and all was less surreal.

"I did not tell you to come," he proclaimed and later, "What will you tell at home?"

"The truth?" she asked in return.

He nodded like a tired man, tired by non-truths, by truths that caught up, truths that tired like long walks on uphill terrain or a heart attack. "Go home," he advised, "Go home and wait for the divorce papers."

Struggling to scrape off the gum stuck at the heel of her new sandal, she managed a shake of her head. "Bigamists can't divorce. You can, of course, financially compensate. I will be with him," she said, pointing a thumb at the boy, ignoring the baffled expression on both faces before her.

"Address it to Amaravati … just Amaravati, no surname."

HAPPY NEW YEAR

The little boy fished out some matter from his eye before ringing the next doorbell. The last house had been a flop. Mrs Kumaraswamy therein had stared at him nonplussed, wearing on her hip a deeply unhappy baby with visible potential for deeper unhappiness. When he announced his request for donation, Mrs Kumaraswamy said something long and throaty in Tamil, which strangely soothed him despite the clarity of her refusal.

"Illa," she told him, shaking her hand and head, providing the baby with an excuse for excessive melancholy. So it was with considerable trepidation that he stood at the next door.

When Mrs Bisht opened the door, he looked into two of the angriest eyes he had ever seen. "Aunty, please donate for the happy new year party."

"Tell me one thing," she said, placing two hands on her large hips. "What is so *saala* happy about the new year? You told me happy new year last time too. If the last year was so happy then why do we want to leave it behind for a new year we have not lived in? And call it happy to boot?"

The boy wiped his fingers on his shorts and repeated more meekly, "This is for the party downstairs, aunty. You don't have to give anything if you don't want to come for it."

She looked back into her house. "I am just coming," said she, making back into the house.

Brightened by the prospects of adding to his kitty, the boy prepared to explore a nostril.

But she came back immediately and empty-handed. "He wants to know who is at the door. Deaf as anything if he does not want to hear something, alert to all he doesn't have to."

The boy smiled politely. He knew who she was talking about. Her husband was the thin uncle-ji who waved his stick at them when they played cricket. The boy had seen him serenely cross roads, not caring about the urgent traffic bearing down on him with screechy brakes. How do they know he is deaf, the boy used to marvel.

"Come inside," she invited.

At once he went in. There were agreeable smells wafting from the kitchen, and a strong curiosity about other people's interiors propelled him in.

She went into the kitchen and came back with a small steel bowl and still no money in sight.

"Here, have some sevai kheer."

He took the bowl from her. There were bits of saffron floating on the milky sweet.

"Only two holidays this month." She clicked her teeth, staring behind him at a calendar on the wall. "There is Id and Republic Day. Still, that's more than some months."

He nodded uncertainly. At six, he got to skip school if his tummy hurt or ear ached. So official holidays were beyond his immediate concern.

"But nothing for your happy new year, eh?" she asked with a sly smile. "No holiday for that. Of course, some drunks will lie the next day about sleeping or vomiting and take a CL or SL. But no government holiday."

He put the bowl down and wiped his chin at places he felt sticky. "Okay then," he said in a sudden fit of generosity, "If you don't want to celebrate, then you don't have to give money."

"Who said I won't celebrate? Just because I say it is not going to be happy, it is still another year, right? And no one knows how it will turn out. I tell you, every one wants a change on January first. The year makes no difference except that it marks time. It is like the train is going to reach your station soon and these years are all the minor stations in between. You start to pack your bags then, isn't it, when your station is about to arrive?"

He nodded enthusiastically in preparation to leave.

"So here," she said, delving two fat fingers into her blouse and coming out with a twenty-rupee note to his wide-eyed wonder. No wonder her chest was so puffed up, he thought. It was made of money!

"Before you go, tell uncle-ji."

He hopped across to the open veranda where he had earlier seen the back of uncle-ji's head above the armchair.

"Uncle-ji…" the boy began. Then he turned to his hostess, "He is fast asleep."

"Wake him up," she said in a voice that brooked no argument.

"UNCLE-JI," he shouted and looked back at her questioningly. He had nothing meaningful to impart to this sleeping man, after all.

She did not move toward them, but nodded intensely. "It is time for his medicines, anyway. Shake him if you want."

Uncle-ji slid to the floor at first shake.

"Oooh," she wailed. "He is dead. He was talking just a minute ago, wasn't he?" she looked at the boy and the boy nodded slowly. He couldn't exactly remember anything, but her grief was too loud, too voluble, too exacting to entertain such trivialities, he felt. Neighbors had begun to walk in by then and he nodded as she asked him this again and again at every new arrival until he began to contribute details of what he had heard the old man say.

"Really?" his mother, who had also arrived on the spot, asked. "He really blessed you before going?"

He said yes, Uncle-ji had.

"They know, you know," his mother said importantly to the people gathered. "People usually know when they are going."

Basking in the glow of his mother's smile and people's clamour, he glanced once more at Uncle-ji on the floor. Someone had put him on his back. Aunty sat next to him on the floor, addressing the corpse. "You made sure there is going to be no happy new year for me," she was saying.

AN INDIAN DIVORCE

I've heard Grace Auntie went deaf and blind when I was still a baby. It seems one fine day she just stopped seeing and hearing. Once she walked into the toilet and went about her ablutions despite her father-in-law's presence. Now why the twin affliction wasn't discovered earlier and why the toilet door wasn't locked were not questions you asked when you were still lisping.

We only knew that Auntie used to sit by the window and smile serenely at the sunlight streaming in. The strange part was the doctor's verdict. "Nothing physically wrong with her," it was said and that's when the word "mad" came to be associated with her.

"Nobody but our Stalin will suffer uncomplainingly like this," I have heard other aunts say. Uncle Stalin, my mother's eldest brother and Grace Auntie's spouse, never dumped his mad wife, the good man that he was.

It was much later in life that I envied her ability at dual handicaps.

I am what you'd call marrried and not go far wrong. It means I have blurred photographs of a wedding reception, assorted jewelry, pretentiously titled heirlooms, one of which tightens menacingly around finger while another spectacularly strangles neck, and was launched into matrimonial space along with handpicked partner to the accompaniment of hired band. A belief in the existence of a single uniting force, a kind of long-living adhesive that would stick us Siamese spouses at the hip, namely love – a dangerous and foolhardy thing to attempt while in orbit – rapidly turned to disbelief.

No doubt love cut a pure path. But what was unclear up until that point was our individual suitability to it and each other. Sure love cut a pure path, but for hitchhikers in us, firmly credulous that road accidents happened to *others*, thumbs were pioneer casualties.

"Arranged marriage?" Friends asked once upon a time, "You have agreed to an arranged marriage?"

I smiled superiorly. Behind the ass-cupping jeans and matte lip-gloss, I was incurably traditional. Conventions could be pooh-poohed for the sake of fashion, but I couldn't commit myself to something as profound as matrimony on a hormonal whim. Besides, most of the men who turned to me with bright stars in their eyes were with fat wives in their basements.

I was set on an irreversible path; that of unlimited goodness and light. And the light nearly blinded me when I smiled sweetly at the ophthalmologically-challenged audience. "Yes, arranged!"

I found their ridiculous boyfriends, self-conscious outings and amateurish amour such contrived happiness. I, on the other hand, would be good and proper and all goodness and propriety would be returned to me with interest.

Therefore, I swept aside all potential soul-mates and jumped bang into the middle of this, believing as I jumped that I was upholding some great Indian tradition. Because, let's face it, divorce statistics are so low here, compared to the debauched West. Three or four husbands, chee-chee. Come, let's marry just once and grin and bear it forever and forever.

The children were on the swings. I was required to look up when they squealed and applaud their scaling of heights. Rosy, the hired help, pushed with a deadpan expression. She would push and I would smile, it had been tacitly agreed upon because I was the mother and she the maid. In an hour, my husband would be home and the tea would be made.

Then the children sat with their books and I was careful not to point out too many mistakes or throw a fit at their retarded replies, like we did in the afternoons, when he wasn't there and we were free to be ourselves and not figments of his imagination.

In the park then, between the forthcoming tea and the hazy incoherence of the day past, I'd blink and daydream. Even if my son scraped his knee or daughter got into a wrangle, I'd unfailingly return to the self-imposed blankness.

That day a strange man stared at me. He was with a little boy and each time the boy acted up, he'd be warned about his mother's anger or arrival. I grew self-conscious, sucking in my stretch-marked stomach and mildly resenting this descent into real life. My unwashed hair, my feet with their cracked open heels ... should've worn that black shirt that didn't stick so, oh but that's put for the wash. I hadn't had to tackle male curiosity for such a long while.

Restless, I replaced Rosy and began to push the swing while she inspected the sky. He sidled closer – his son was on the twin swing – and we pushed together, higher and higher until our children squealed. For some reason I was reminded of the religious ceremony ten years ago, when I had stood at the side of another man, welding into a wedding.

This, too, seemed as solemn and ritualistic; he would push, then I would push. Silent and rhythmic and senseless but necessary, publicly sanctioned gestures in the larger context just like that day, except that my bladder wasn't full and face cream did not melt down my neck under a harsh video light.

I withstood the stranger's frank stare as long as I could until an involuntary smile jettisoned my facial muscles.

Very, very softly, his voice folding in sandy hillocks of inquiry and infatuation, he commented, "Your eyes, they look so sad."

And I shivered with pleasant apprehension and kept my eyes modestly down. When my son kissed me, a small, insect-bite of a kiss on the way home, I blushed.

Later, I made my husband his tea and in that short respite between homework and dinner, I gingerly picked up the park incident, which I had tucked away like some deliciously illicit secret at the back of my mind, to examine and exult in. "Your eyes, they look so sad. Your eyes, they look so sad. Youreyestheylooksosad…."

There I was among the carefully arranged ornaments and artful mirror-work cushions in my own familiar drawing room, stimulated by a stranger's comment. This made me vaguely guilty and to get rid of it and to stress my own innocence, I told my husband about the incident.

"What a cliché!" he muttered and immediately I tried to look like I knew it all the while, those cheats with their arsenal of compliments on the prowl for some horny housewife.

Where is the sharp woman I used to be?

In the church basement, I watched a woman who couldn't keep her legs together due to the advanced state of her pregnancy. I heard the priest commend her for her fidelity to a man somewhere in the Gulf spreading cheer and HIV.

"He has AIDS," she murmured to me, but with no sense of enjoyment in his malady. The fear of her own fatality was in her eye. Mutely, she had nodded at whatever the priest said and the priest did say a lot of sensible things.

But when he turned to me, like her and like Grace Auntie, I adopted the speech of the damned – silence.

For how does one say: "I want an annullment."

Behind me were the real victims, those whose husbands beat them or raped their daughters. But the counsellor was kind to me.

"What do you want to change in your marriage?" he asked.

I wanted to say, "Everything." The marriage. The husband. The long wait for the marriage to begin....

But I said nothing.

My own father had said: "Come now, you know what's an annullment. That's what Philo's daughter got when she saw her husband's genitals for the first time, so much like a girl's. There is legal validity attached to such a de-linking. But what you speak is nonsense. It will make you a laughing stock!"

I have two children, you see, and it is obvious I am not a virgin. Annullments are for those married to lunatics or impotent men. Those who can't or won't. Not someone like me who has been married for x number of years, publicly multiplied twice, drops her children to school, eats up her husband's earnings. No, not for someone like me at all. I can apply only for divorce, which is an admission of being married in the first place.

"All husbands are workaholics. Why do you want to separate really?" An old classmate asked slyly.

I was fed, watered, shod and sexed, they said. I was being looked after. There was the man who lent me his name, not asking a bit of my own name in return.

So I came back to my happy home, having asked the church not for a controversial annulment, but prayers for my doubting Thomas soul. I lit a candle at Mother Mary's shrine so I wouldn't start or peer blankly when addressed. Especially by a man called Husband.

Mother's statue mutely stared back and I remembered her platonic marriage, her unchallenged chastity. Same pinch, her stone eyes seemed to say till I wanted to blurt words of comfort to her.

For I want to be done thinking about me. The me

I sense here and there, the me I try to stifle under the dirty laundry or stirring gravy, the me as irksome and attention seeking as a missed period.

On the one hand my children are growing up – I relish. On the other hand, parents are ageing – I worry. In between, there is this stranger. Lurking in the mirror, in some happy woman's laugh, in a movie poster, in the pages of a book. Naively I had thought let me address her first and then get on. But she disappears the minute I look.

Sitting down for dinner with husband, children and father-in-law, I realized what my aunt had discovered long ago before me. How a marriage can also be a divorce. How a marriage did not automatically follow a marriage ceremony. How one can feel married to every single man in the world except the one yoked to self.

Grace Auntie, the bashful bride of Brightness, wed to the sunlight that poured in through a broken window to caress her care-worn face into a thousand tanned hickeys, to converse in shades of light all day long and to steal away at night with tender promises of dawn.

And me? I still have to identify a groom.

A Fairy Tale

Witch (with basket atop head): Poisoned apples! Poisoned apples! Oh, I mean, apples, just plain and simple apples without *any* poison.

Snow White (with a coy smile): Can I sell you some acne cream instead? It is homemade. Also, there's something for your er ... darkness. You cannot become as fair as me, of course, but you can be less like the bottom of a burnt pan. And this, this will take care of your hairy warts.

Witch: I have come to sell, not buy, if you don't mind. I am retailer, not socialite.

Sno: Oh, okay. Give me some apples, you old hag.

(The witch puts her basket down).

Sno: There is only one apple in this and it is neither red nor juicy.

Witch (sotto voce): Well, how many apples does she expect an old woman to sit and poison?

Sno: What?

Witch: And I thought I was the deaf one. (Loudly) I said my apple tree is drying.

Sno: I'll bite. How much is it?

Witch: Fifty-five rupees.

Sno: I don't have that kind of money. Dwarfs are little people, how much work do you think they can do with their tiny little hands?

Witch: I meant fifty-five paise. Just buy it, will you?

Sno: Thank you. (Takes a bite) Mmmm, this is so good, I feel I am in heaven.

Witch: It will send her there all right. Ha ha (the evil laugh).

The witch stands in a corner as Snow White chokes and falls to the ground.

The dwarfs march in.

First dwarf: This Snow White is always sleeping.

Second: Lazy bum.

Third: And that too outside the house.

Fourth: Hey, I think she's dead.

Fifth: How do you know?

Sixth: She isn't snoring.

Seventh (checking Sno's pulse): Yep. She is dead.

All seven: Let's bury her.

A prince wanders in.

Prince: I am the Handsome Prince. Here, it says so in my bio-data. I kiss dead princesses ... I know it is a dirty job, but someone's gotta do it. Leaves my lips dry though. Oh, for some chap stick. (Sees Snow White) What's this? Another dead damsel. Falling about like dead flies all of them. She must have known I'd be passing this way.

(He leans toward Snow White)

First dwarf: Er ... Mr. Prince, if you don't mind, we prefer her like this.

Second: A bit silent.

Third (covering his ears): Goes yak, yak, yak all the time.

Fourth: Banging pots and pans.

Fifth: Complaining of headaches *every* night.

Sixth: She suits us best this way.

Seventh: A bit dead.

Prince: Alice-in-Fuckland, this is my job! Are you offering me VRS?

Dwarfs (pulling out fourteen empty pockets): Go ahead, we are broke.

Prince bends toward Snow White.

Prince (choking): Oooh, bad breath, bad breath. (Falls down)

Witch (disappointed): What do you know, she was Sleeping Beauty!

Moral of the story: Never waste good poison.

THE SHORT AND THE SHORT OF IT

I would have bitten off his head but I dared not make him shorter. He was quite easily the shortest man in the whole world. An astrologer in Amritsar had read his horoscope and told him: "Have your head bitten off. That is sure to make you grow into the tallest man on earth. But mind you, the head should come off in one single bite."

"I don't believe it," he had recounted to me with the most modest of smiles. "I can never become the tallest man in the world. The tallest man in Punjab, yes. The tallest man in Asia, perhaps. But nah, not the tallest man in the world."

From then on he has been pestering me with demands to bite his head off.

It is a bizarre request, I told him patiently at first.

It could be painful I warned later. Besides, the police will not look kindly on such an act. Secretly, I feared he would not be able to explain my seemingly cannibalistic fit without a head to house a tongue that could talk in the first place.

"Bite my head off," he tells me in all seriousness. "Just bite it off."

For some reason, he thinks I can do that. Bite his silly head off. That in one single swallow my teeth can sweep his head off his neck.

In vain have I tried to fob him off, to distract, to dissuade, alternately gently and sternly. But he remains determined in his decision to lose head, gain height.

"What if your head does not come off in one bite?" I'd ask him, catching him in between his routine pleas to be dentally decapitated. "Or worse, hangs by a messy tendon or two?"

Nope, he shook his head, (yes, the same head he wants orally guillotined).

I found him to be impervious to dramatic threats, subtle entreaties and even moving poetic prose in defence of his erstwhile stature.

He thought of himself as a blade of grass or a length of human hair that would grow if snipped a bit.

"I dreamt," he told me once mistily, "that my head bumped in the clouds. That birds warbled in my nostrils."

"Just a dream," I hurriedly dismissed.

"Yes," he beamed. "Imagine eggs in my ears! No one can be that tall."

"Too much of anything can be a very, very bad thing," I backtracked alas too late.

He came home once carrying a stool.

"What's this?" I asked, hoping he'd upholstered a compromise with the cosmic powers of vertical extensions.

"Just want to get used to heights," he said, climbing solemnly on to the stool. "The sudden rise in altitude shouldn't dizzy me, right, when it happens?"

Oh, he'd thought of all the angles, I despaired, watching him manoeuvre skilfully stools and stilts through traffics and crowds.

"What if you die?" I asked. For he can get away with death easier than I could with murder.

Or I'd pull his leg. "Learn yoga, levitate."

Finally, one grey winter evening, I gave up. "Okay," I surrendered. "Tell me when. Tell me where and I'll be there with my teeth on."

He gazed at me somewhat emotionally and embarrassingly.

On the appointed day, we met. The auspicious moment had to be, we were told, neither dawn nor dusk, neither in nor out, neither in home clothes nor in formalwear.

So, we gazed at each other at ten minutes to five a.m. in his roofed veranda, attired in housecoats made entirely of silk ties.

At the strike of five, he advanced toward me. I stood still, surreptitiously sharpening my molars, pre-molars, my incisors, and even my wisdom teeth, which are the shy retiring types.

He stood before me and bowed like an ancient Japanese warrior seen in TV ads. I bared my teeth and the dim light rippled over my canines with a blinding glint, like in another TV ad.

Then I slowly stretched up on my toes because, well I forgot to add, I am shorter than him. He is the shortest man in the world, but I am a woman and therefore technically only the shortest woman in the world.

Back to the moment, back to the moment, please. I arched, he bent and then a strange thing happened. We kissed.

After marriage, we joined the Great Indian Circus where all his practice with stilts has stood us in good stead.

"The prophecy has come true," he never tires of telling me with the most tender of smiles as he readies to elevate on the stilts. "Your love's put me at the top of the world!"

Since then, quite simply, we've been walking on air.

THE BIRIYANI BITCHES

I would be asked, if people felt inclined to include me in the conversation, why I was in this business, the body business.

Because, I tell them, pulling a long face, I have no money to call my own. So I don't call my body my own. I know it won't last, this demand for me, so I am doing what entrepreneurs do, deliver till stock lasts.

My customers are nice people who like to think I am not doing it for money but purely for pleasure, a pleasure I am paid to manufacture and exaggerate for the bill commensurates. In this business, one learns early to reach out eagerly for the foul-breathed, flabby, flatulent men.

I rely on word-of-mouth recommendations to attend "bachelor" parties, which are basically a bunch of balding men getting together to bitch about their wives and boast about conquests. I sit with them and shiver – my dress code more informal than theirs – while they lambaste spouses, secretaries and servants. I am careful to add ice regularly to my drink so they don't keep filling my glass. For they may want to relax, indeed they kindly keep exhorting me to "relax, baby" but I am on duty, like the bottle of Scotch whiskey or the plate of sheekh kebabs. We don't retire until the last drop dries or an onion ring remains.

Sometimes I dance awkwardly and they clap and cheer me on.

They talk about their children, too, who are studying abroad or writing sensitive poetry, idly stroking my head or thigh, postponing my role so as to get their money's worth of me. Then they order biriyanis, which is my cue and the pungent smell of spices makes me sick.

As their hands – eight in all – randomly pluck, a million mice crawl over me. At this time, I try to get the arithmetic right and add different tips to the sum, arriving at interesting differentials. I allow myself a dream or two, keeping my dreams small for fear of constipated sleep.

Sometimes this part is the best, though physically so exhausting I could sleep forever. I feel in power at last. They may have fancy wives who go for meditation and pottery classes, but I am the one they mould with such urgent worship.

The end is mercifully quick and they are seldom mean with money as they outdo each other in footing the bill or impressing the boss. But as they pay, they begin to detach. Sated by my sweat, these men now turn to each other, picking up conversation where left off; about the same wives, the same pottery classes, the same meditation centers.

The wives and pots are their real world while I am the rented space. Sometimes, the tipping is nasty with wads of notes – ten rupee ones bunched together to suggest bulk – thrust into my hands like I am a beggar on the street. This is accompanied by endearments of their choice, addressed simultaneously to my father or brother. While paying, they take care not to brush my contaminated skin, the same skin they suckled just seconds ago. Thank you, I say, nevertheless. For they may return or recommend and while they may be moody, money is money.

Now they are in a hurry to leave and protocol and pimp demand I play hostess. So I hang back, still smiling while they beep their drivers and depart one by one into the night.

For a few minutes, between my auto-driver's arrival and their going, I am alone in the room. The chairs, the beds, the curtains, the A/C, flat sodas, soggy peanuts and me. Often the driver finds me squatting on the floor and enjoying the remains of the feast. I laugh and talk in long sentences to myself. Sometimes, despite the soreness, I even dance.

Shinie Antony, who lives in Delhi, wishes she were anywhere else.
"A Dog's Death," included in this collection, won the Commonwealth Broadcasting Association (Asia) award for short-story writing, in 2002. "Kiss and Tell" was previously published in *The Statesman* in 2003.